Ruaun3

Also by Jane Shoup

Down in the Valley
Spirit of the Valley
Will of the Valley
Knightfall
The Restoration
Zan, Birth of a Legend
The Key
A Choice of Captors
Ammey McKeaf, Book 1~ The Chronicles of Azulland
Heirs to the Throne, Book 2 ~ Chronicles of Azulland
Into Shadow, Book 3 ~ The Chronicles of Azulland
Charity Cases
Santa:2020 The Final Ride
The Time Tunnel of August Kaplan
An American Baroness, Book 1~ Sons of Barons
Nearly a Marquess, Book 2 ~ Sons of Barons
London's Adonis, Book 3 ~ Sons of Barons
Christmas at Manoria, Book 4, Sons of Barons
The Stewart Women, Book 5, Sons of Barons
Manley Georgine

Copyright © 2024 by Jane Shoup
ISBN: 979-8-9908944-2-6

.

1

So this is me … on autopilot

Picture an average-looking seventeen-year-old guy, glassy eyed from sitting in front of a computer at night and, sadly, you've pretty well got me pegged. In my darkened bedroom with only the light of the screen illuminating my face, I had to have looked more than a little zombie-like as the clock at the bottom of the computer screen changed to one a.m. One a.m., Wednesday, January 30, 2008. What a depressing sounding date, right? I needed to crash and get some sleep, so I stretched my neck, rolled my shoulders and pressed **New Game.**

Why, a logical person might ask? Good question, especially since I had school in a matter of hours, and I didn't even want to play anymore. But I was on autopilot.

Sirena, one of the supremely gorgeous females of Ruaun3, appeared on the screen, as always, and said, "Choose your level," in a warning and yet seductive tone and with a decidedly defiant expression.

I pressed 5.

"Choose which side you will take," Sirena commanded with a lift of her chin.

I cursored to Hood and hit enter. As if I'd be Foundation.

"Choose which of us will represent you."

The cast of Hoods appeared on screen, and I circled the mouse around before choosing Ji for one last go round. Although, to be honest, I'd mentally pledged that for the last several games.

It's not that I have to be all that alert in school, but actual slumbering in class leaves a less than favorable impression, while my preference is not to leave an impression at all. Teachers would collectively tell you I'm a polite kid who does well academically. My GPA is a 4.0, although that score is bogus because the school I attended for the first year and half of high school didn't have AP classes, which everyone knows is how you load a GPA.

From whom I inherited intelligence is the real question. It either had to be some long-ago descendant or, going a little esoteric here, it's left over from a previous incarnation. Like how some individuals are born musical prodigies. I saw an interview once where this musical genius kid claimed that full symphonies just came to him and all he had to do was to scribble down the notes. I lean toward the second option, because intelligence was not passed down from my mother or father or their mothers or fathers, which seems like a definite trend.

I don't remember my dad, but I've learned enough about him from pictures and stories to know he was no prodigy of any sort. He drowned surfing twelve-foot waves while stoned. At the time of his demise, he delivered pizza for a living. To be fair to my parents, they were both seventeen when my mom became pregnant, and most seventeen-year-olds are not known for savvy decision making. Then, again, I'm seventeen. Seventeen going on thirty-eight, according to my mom, but she would say that.

On the screen, a dozen gnarly looking assassins approached my avatar with bloodlust in their eyes, and Ji was already in rough shape from the last fight. I hit Pause and then cursered over to Quit and clicked.

See? Not that hard.

I practically creaked as I unfolded myself from the chair. Who wouldn't after sitting in the same position for four hours straight? My obsessive game play is nothing but a quest for escape from my water-flavored life. At least, I'm aware of it, if that counts for anything.

I hit the bed, ready for unconsciousness, and stared at the rotating ceiling fan as my thoughts flitted from game tactics to my chemistry homework to the essay I still need to write for one of my college applications. If I'd been born into a family of means, I'd already be in college. Instead, I skipped a couple of years of school because the one where we lived at the time was *that* bad. So I home schooled myself. No kidding, although it was a total joke.

I literally dropped off the accountability grid and skipped part of fourth, all of fifth and part of sixth grade. Then we moved again and landed in a decent school district. Then, even though I was tested and placed significantly beyond it, The Powers That Be chose to put me into sixth grade, claiming I would be more likely to succeed socially.

Right.

So now I'm only in the fifth inning of my junior year. My plan is to have everything ready for college's early consideration next fall. I want to get far away from this place and everyone I've ever known, and I want an answer as to where that will be as soon as possible. Then I can start really counting down days, which is one of the things I do best in life.

Nothing against mom, but I need a clean slate, and one of my own choosing this time. My SAT scores will be good enough to get me noticed, but I'll probably need a killer essay too since I don't have a stellar GPA or any school or community achievements or involvement to trumpet.

Sleep finally began nibbling away at consciousness, but then I jerked awake, afraid that I'd forgotten to set the alarm. Surprisingly, it was 5:30 in the morning. Not so surprisingly, I hadn't forgotten to set the alarm because I was cursed with a responsibility gene. I threw my arm over my eyes and tried to decide if I had to pee too badly to go back to sleep. That's when a title for my essay occurred to me. *Seventeen years of being a slacker*. I rolled onto my side and struggled for the first few words, that elusive first sentence.

We're all products of our parents to some degree.

No. Lame. And not true, either.

I worked to clear and open my mind since I believe that inspiration can be drawn from something beyond what we see. If that statement is unsettling, you should know I have more than a few unconventional beliefs. For one thing, I feel seriously displaced in time. I've always felt I belonged somewhere and sometime different from this. Maybe in the early middle ages, the era of knights. In the long-ago days of early post-Roman domination, almost any young man who wanted to could go into the service of a nobleman and become a knight.

Because there was no established government-type protection at the time, knights protected and defended their noble's land and all the people who lived on it. Initially, they were paid in the currency of the day. Later, they were often given grants of land, which was better since they could make income off that land.

What eventually happened was the land grants were passed from father to firstborn son along with their knighthood and, in so doing, knights grew to not only think of themselves, but to make themselves into an elevated class far way above commoners. By medieval times, if you were not the son of knight, it was nearly impossible to become one. It's sad that money always rules.

Another of my unconventional beliefs is that I love this one particular girl. I haven't even met her, but I know that I will know her when I see her. Sometimes, between sleep and wakefulness, this glimpse of her teasingly surfaces from the depth of my subconscious. I try to hang on to it, but I can't. The only things I know for sure is that she is magnificent, she has beautiful eyes, even though I don't know what color, and she has the most adorable dimples when she smiles. Naturally, I don't tell anyone these notions of mine. Then again, I really don't tell anybody much of anything.

I'm *Mister Invisible*. It's a decent title.

The reasons behind being invisible, I mentally edit.

Reason one. Seven different schools in eleven years. I am the product of a single mom who believes in geographical cures. Life sucks, no decent men around to date, hate the dead-end job? Move! I would never cast her as a villain, because she's not. She wouldn't have chosen the shit luck she's had in life.

Plus which, she could have bailed and started over without me at any time. As far as I know, she never even considered it.

It's true she drinks too much, cusses like a drunken, pissed off sailor a lot of the time, and sleeps around pretty freely. But, to her credit, she's never brought a man home until she thought it might turn into something serious. It's not her fault she's an optimist. I've seen her go though a Phillip, a Chuck, a John, two Jeff's, a Chris, a Ricardo, a Ben, a Steve and a Howie, plus there's a few to whom I can't affix a name. Sadly, but predictably, the end result of her love affairs is always the same. If the guy doesn't break up with her in a couple of months, she shuts down cold because they aren't the deceased, nineteen-year-old pothead, pizza-delivery love of her life.

I've often wondered if my folks were high when they named me. Not that my first name, Matthew, is anything but common, but it becomes an unusual choice when one's surname is Matthews. Role calls are such a joy.

I dozed back off only to be reawakened by the alarm. I was dazed with exhaustion, but also relieved to be torn from the creepy, recurrent dream I'd just experienced for the fifth or sixth time. The dream seems eerily real. I'm rushing down a hall at school because something terrible is happening. I'm either right in the middle of it or maybe I'm the cause of it. No one except me is in the hall. I look in a room as I pass and a thin girl in a red t-shirt reaching out to shut the door. She sees me and freezes, she's so freaked. And so am I.

I sat and swung my legs around, seriously considering skipping school. The thought lasted about thirty seconds before I dragged my ass to the bathroom. I showered, got ready and headed to the kitchen feeling heavy and dull, the result of not sleeping enough for too many consecutive nights in a row. If only there was someone else to blame for that.

Surprisingly, Mom was up. I say surprisingly because she is very, very not a morning person. Then I realized she was wearing the clothes she'd had on yesterday. "Late night?" I asked.

She grunted.

She was reading a newspaper which is also not a common occurrence. "Since when do we get the paper?" I asked as I poured myself a bowl of store-brand sugar-coated corn flakes.

"Probably a new paper kid or something," she muttered.

She always mutters when she's lying. I sat at the table as she flipped the page. That's when I saw the headline and the reason she'd swiped a neighbor's newspaper.

THIRD TEEN MURDER.

"Shit," I breathed. I saw the name of my school and leaned closer, experiencing a tightening in my gut. "It's somebody from North?"

She set down the paper with a heavy sigh. "Yeah." What was left of yesterday's makeup wasn't looking so good. "They're not releasing her name yet, but she was a sophomore. A damned sophomore in high school," she said with an incredulous expression. "What a fucked-up world." She rose and started for the door. "I'm taking a shower."

I reached for the paper and devoured the article. It was mostly about the first two victims, Kaci Smith, a seventeen-year-old senior from West Washington High and Ellyn Lamb, a fifteen-year-old who'd been home-schooled all her life. This was the third murder of a pretty, wholesome, teenage girl within the school year. *Wholesome* was a description the media used frequently. Three victims this school year and it was only the end of January.

What I really wanted to do was to crawl back into bed and sleep. Instead, I pulled my shit together and left. There was no point in saying bye to Mom since she couldn't have heard over the shower and the radio blaring hits of the eighties, the only music she considers worthy of listening to.

I walk to school for three reasons. I'm close enough, I don't have a car, and there is no way I'm riding the bus. I've saved enough over the years to buy a cheap car, but I can't swing the insurance too and neither can Mom. The payments would wipe me out and I don't know what kind of college expenses I'll have. Priorities are priorities. I have four months, one week and three days until the close of my junior year. Then summer and then one more school year before I'm out of here. I have the rest of my life to buy a car.

Being poor has always been a pain in the ass, but it's about to come in handy for the first time because we should qualify for financial aid. Between that and a scholarship or two, I should be okay.

The words *should be okay*, glare in my mind. I suddenly wondered if Kaci Smith, Ellyn Lamb and Victim Three had thought the same thing.

2

My Preferred World: Ruaun3

It was gray and freezing as I walked home from school that day. Once I got inside, I went through my daily routine. I kicked up the temperature on the thermostat, pulled on a sweatshirt, booted up my antiquated desktop computer, and went in search of sustenance. I devoured the last of some generic Crunch and Munch, which was beyond stale, and then hit the bathroom.

In first block, the announcement had been made that Victim Three was a girl named Madison Perry, which caused a big shock. There were gasps and tears, and most of it seemed legit. The principal spoke over the intercom about tragedy striking our school and said that trained counselors were available in the guidance office for anyone who felt the need to talk. He then called for a minute of silence. I didn't time it, but that minute felt like it lasted a long friggin' time.

One second.

Two.

Three.

There was a choked sound and then a girl burst into fresh tears.

First block finally ended and most of us headed toward second. It's weird the way tragedy makes people connect. Even me and I'm invisible. Kids made eye contact they don't normally make. I got nodded at and spoken to as if inclusion was the order of the day. As the day went on, photos of Madison sprang up everywhere. Everyone was talking about her. She was pretty and petite with shoulder-length brown hair. A cheerleader. Popular. Really nice. I must have heard, 'really nice' a dozen times. I'd never met Madison but, by the end of the day, I felt her absence, as weird as that may sound.

The only way I can explain it is like this. Imagine walking into a big room that's decorated perfectly, except for there's this one space that's devoid of anything. Then a tour guide tells you there used to be a statue there of a beautiful goddess that was warm to the touch and made people feel good, but it had been stolen. You've never seen it or anything like it, but now it seems like it should be there. It feels wrong that's not there.

No more thinking, I decided as I sat at my desk. I took a drink of flat generic root beer and launched New Game. I'm currently level five of eight of the revised version of Ruaun3. I made it all the way to eight in the original, but the new one is more challenging.

The original Sirena had light blonde hair and wore a tight, slightly off the shoulders top that, in my humble opinion, looked more Daisy in Dukes of Hazzard than rebel vixen in 2813. In the revised version, Sirena's hair is darker worn in a blunt cut above her shoulders. Her outfit is different but still tight, which works for me. Someone put concentrated effort into her D-cups, which is nice work if you can get it.

In case you don't know the story of Ruaun3, it's this. Earth became uninhabitable around 2500 AD after too many greenhouse gases did too much damage to Earth's atmosphere allowing solar radiation to essentially fry the earth. When it became obvious that Earth's demise was inevitable, there was a scramble to build life-sustaining biodomes for the surface of the doomed planet, other planets and even the floor of the ocean. As they grew larger in scale, some proved successful, others a tragic bust.

The great breakthrough of the age was the creation of a dwarf planet called Napricus. It was a game changer. Its atmosphere was contained, so it supported life. Rather than serve as a life raft, it became a new beginning. It was no earth, but it was habitable. Others soon followed.

Fast forward a few hundred years and hundreds of worlds have been created, naturally some more desirable than others. Enter the bad guys, aka The Foundation, an intergalactic organization that amassed enough power to take over the governmental administrations of many planets.

In 2808, The Foundation swooped into Ruaun3 and began what they called qualified forced removals, or QFRs, of anyone designated as 'adversative.' Basically, they were accepting bids from the wealthy of other planets and biodomes who preferred living on Ruaun3 and moving out as many citizens of Ruaun3 as they needed to accommodate the new arrivals. As you can imagine, a resistance sprung up. The rebel force is referred to as Hoods.

So, the premise of the game is that the Hoods fight on despite a constant battle to survive against the ruthless and powerful Foundation. Some of the key players, besides Sirena, are Smoke who is knock-out gorgeous with a single silver streak in her otherwise blue-black hair, Teddy is Smoke's man, and he is as handsome as she's beautiful. Dairy, a woman of thirty or so, has short, spiky, platinum hair and violet eyes. She is kick-ass tough. Gabe and Westin are twins who might have been Abercrombie models in our time. Aiden, the leader, is a muscular, dark-skinned black man with a deep, commanding voice. There are half a dozen more notable hoods in the game besides the above mentioned.

On the opposing side, you have Cutter, a cold-hearted son of a bitch with movie star looks and great mystique. There's also a heavy-set British dude they called Letters who appears now and again, but no one can play as him or Cutter. There are always a lot of FO's, Foundation Officers, in skirmishes and raids, but they're never identified by name and they have pretty much generic features. If you opt to play as a Foundation operative, you create your own avatar. Name, physical characteristics, all of it.

The huntress is one of the most mysterious characters in the game. She only comes when bidden and *if* you can afford to hire her, whatever side you choose. She is not cheap, but she always seems to possess answers no one else has. She's striking with short dark hair, a pert nose and a conceited expression. Also worthy of mention are the Veorwulfe, a vicious, animal-like race who are allied with The Foundation. Otherwise known as the assassins of Mount Veorwithe. There were no Veorwulfe on Ruaun3 until The Foundation took over.

End of explanation. When my cell phone rang that afternoon, or what I thought was still afternoon before I saw it was after six, I knew it was Mom calling. Like it's ever anyone else. "Hi, Mom."

"What'cha doing?" she asked.

"Homework."

By the way, that's not a lie, technically speaking. I was at home and Ruaun3 is what I work at.

"I was thinking I might go out with the girls after work."

And? I thought. She typically goes out three or four days a week and I'm sure it would be more if money permitted.

"Did you eat yet?"

"No. I was just going to go get something."

"There's leftover pizza."

I've grown to detest pizza because we have it so much. "Yeah, I'll probably have that," I said anyway. It's commonly known as the path of least resistance.

"Okay. I won't be late."

Puhleeze. I think the last time I waited up, I was nine and she was pissed. "'Kay."

"How was it today?"

I sat back and ran a hand through my hair. "It was pretty intense," I admitted. "They announced who Victim Three was."

"I know. It's on the news, too. Did you know her?"

"No."

"It's so awful, isn't it?"

I found myself nodding and thinking about it again, which is exactly what I didn't want to do. "Yeah, it sucks."

"You're okay though, right?"

"Yeah, I'm okay," I said flatly.

A beat of silence. "Because I could come home."

Except she didn't want to and, besides, what would we do except sit around and watch TV? "Seriously, I'm okay," I said more believably.

11

"Well, okay. If you're sure. Go eat something, okay?"

For some reason, the thought of me eating always assuages her guilt. Not that there's a lot of guilt, mind you. She's not a big believer in the concept. "I will. No worries. Have fun."

True to my word, I took a break from the game and dined on two cans of generic ravioli. I pondered doing a load of laundry but went back to the game instead. A little after eleven, I thought about hanging it up and going to bed. At twelve-thirty, it occurred to me my eyes stung like holy hell. I started **New Game.** As always, the epic-sounding score played as the story of the game scrolled by. You can skip it at the get-go, but I hadn't been fast enough. "Yada, yada, yada," I murmured as I repeatedly pressed Skip Intro and my computer ignored me.

As always, Sirena appeared on screen. My finger hovered over 5 as I waited for, "Choose your level," but the words didn't come. I let an expletive slip thinking it was frozen, but something was off. Sirena seemed to be looking at me with her brow was raised in irritation. It felt like she was refusing me another game.

Okay. Obviously, I was brain-fried, so I pressed **End Game.** The onscreen image dissolved, but I continued to sit there like moss on a rock. Finally, I got up because it was late, I was half comatose with exhaustion, and it was possibly I'd just experienced some sort of delusional episode. I'd never given basic sanity all that much thought but, come to think of it, I wanted mine.

When I climbed into bed, sleep eluded me yet again. A person can be too wired to sleep, and I was. I'd start to doze only to jerk wide-awake again. The clock had just struck one when I heard Mom come in, buzzed and singing to herself. Sadly, the woman cannot carry a tune in a bucket. The next sound I heard was my alarm clock. I sprang up weirdly energized from a bizarre dream where I'd been walking with Sirena. When we stopped outside one of the back entrances of my school, the one I always use in the morning, she turned to face me.

"It's time to stop playing, Matt," she said. "Three murdered girls. And there may be more."

What was she talking about? "That doesn't have anything to do with me."

"Yes, it does. You're the only one that can help. Find the huntress."

Find the huntress? "You just said I was supposed to stop playing," I said with a smirk.

She looked confused and then she opened her mouth to reply, but there was only the sound of my damned alarm.

I got out of bed and tried to shrug it off. I mean, why not? Dreams are caused by the brain churning up what you're worrying about and mentally working on, so, obviously, my brain took the ingredients of recent thoughts, mixed them all together and *voila.* It didn't mean anything. It couldn't mean anything.

3

The Populars, the Skunk Club and Graylin

It was drizzling as I got ready for school, so I grabbed my waterproof jacket with hood that doesn't fit right and pulled it over my layered shirts. With the hood in place, I look like your standard garden-variety punk, but I can make it to school in twelve minutes if I run. Once there, I can duck in a back entrance, pull off the jacket and stash it in my locker before anyone has a chance to see me and judge. Avoid judgment when possible. This is my mantra.

Unfortunately, right before I hit the door of our apartment building, a major deluge began. No way was I walking in that, so I leaned against the wall, hoping it would let up. I noticed the rolled-up newspaper in front of a neighbor's door and figured it wouldn't hurt to sneak a peek.

The front page featured three photos of Madison Perry. The first was a standard school picture. The second was a posed cheerleading picture with one pom-pom raised high and the other resting on her hip. The third was a recent family photo of her about to blow out lit candles on a birthday cake. You can tell she's struggling not to smile as she attempts to blow out the candles. Other people are in the background, although you can't see them very well. It was *her* moment, her very alive moment.

I perused the article until I came to the word *wholesome* again. *Anyone heard of a thesaurus?* While the downpour continued, I read the piece and discovered that Madison's body had been found in the girls' locker room of our school. That was creepy. I looked out at the rain recalling what I'd read about the other victims.

The first, Kaci Smith, had been discovered at home in her room by her six-year-old brother. The poor kid was probably scarred for life. How could he not be? The second, Ellyn, was found in a second-floor public bathroom in a mall by a janitor at closing time. The only connections between the victims seemed to be their age, race, the wholesomeness factor and the fact that they'd been strangled – or, more accurately, garroted. I cringed because the thought of being garroted is so freaking gruesome.

I rolled the newspaper back up, finagled the rubber band back around it and put it back where I'd found it, then trudged back upstairs to let Mom know I needed a ride. She was as joyful about driving me as I'd thought she'd be, but I got to school nice and dry with the jacket shoved in my backpack.

I never use the front entrance, but that morning was the exception because it's the only drop off point under a canopy. I felt strange and conspicuous as I made my way through the lobby. I had never experienced such a collective heaviness before. It was like wading through a quicksand of depression. In one group, girls were crying and everyone else seemed close to it. It wasn't pretend, hey-give-me-some-attention crying either. I swallowed hard, tightened my grip on the strap of my book bag and kept walking. I wished I'd been dropped off in back. It would have been better to get soaked than walk through this.

A peel of laughter shocked me into stopping and looking over at the girl it came from. *Goth* was my first thought. She was petite and super hard-core looking, with too much eyeliner and bizarre two-tone hair, half white, half jet-black. It reminded me of a skunk. She was standing with three guys who also had black and white hair. Total stoners. She had on a black T-shirt with 'I'm the One,' emblazoned in sparkly silver studs and she had a multitude of facial piercings.

Her loud amusement while standing right next to people who were sincerely hurting didn't feel like mere insensitivity. It had a more sinister, salt-in-the-wound kind of feel to it. The group's laughter was pissing people off. It even pissed me off and I'm invisible and insulated, just floating by on my way to LAHS, life after high school. I mean, if you want to be a total, fucking jackass, go somewhere else to do it. It's not that hard.

"Hey," a square-jawed jock fumed from within a circle of populars. High school royalty. "I suggest you get far away from us. Like now!"

"Or what, jockstrap?" skunk girl retorted.

This was happening not even ten feet from me.

"It's still a free country," she gloated. "Room for freaks, losers, Disney star wannabes who are sad about their friend—" she made a grotesque mockery of being garroted.

The jock lunged forward, but a couple other guys from his group grabbed and restrained him. "They're not worth it, man," one of them said.

The skunk club had backed up a step, all except skunk girl, who seemed totally in her element. "Whatever," one of the skunks said. "Who needs this funeral shit, anyway?"

"Yeah, fuck it," another said. "Come on."

Skunk girl pursed her lips at the jock who was looking a little like Bruce Banner beginning his transformation into the Hulk, and then led the skunk club right past me, taking up more room than necessary. I realized I'd been staring like everyone else, so I took a deep breath and exhaled, determined to block them and everyone else out for the rest of the day.

Only four months and change, then the summer, then one more year and then I am out of here, I thought as I headed to AP history.

Call me weird, but I enjoy history. It's fascinating to study the 'progress' of humankind. Kings and queens, wars, periods of excess, uprisings, famines, revolutions, genocide, the politics and propaganda. Unfortunately, the teacher, Mrs. Zimmerman was not let in on that fact. She's exceptionally fond of teaching via videotape. The movie that morning was on the fall of the Roman Empire, and it was especially bad even for an educational video. The narrator's monotone lulled unfortunate viewers into a level of boredom that bordered on coma.

I try to always snag a seat in the back of the classroom, usually on the side closest to the door, but in this class, I am stuck in the middle because of assigned seats. Row M. A guy named Alac Munn sits to my right, but he'd made the wise choice to be absent. I mention that because, midway through the video, on the verge of nodding off like most the other kids in class, I noticed someone sitting in Alac's seat, which had been empty when the movie started. I looked over and my jaw dropped to see Sirena sitting there looking at me.

I purposely looked away, blinked and then looked back, locking gazes with the girl one seat over from Alac's empty chair. *Shit.* I looked away again, embarrassed because I'm sure it seemed like I had been staring at her. Or had I been? Sirena wasn't there now and she probably hadn't been at all. No, not probably. *Obviously* Sirena, who is a character in a game, had not just been sitting next to me.

Okay. I must be trying to work out some psychological conflict and Sirena represents some sort of answer. I decided then and there that the game is on hold. Definitely on hold until further notice.

Finally the movie ended as all droning, poorly filmed educational videos will. Zimmerman passed out a study sheet for the upcoming test and class ended. As I made my way to the door, I was aware that the girl I'd accidentally been staring at was too. In fact, she was keeping pace with me one row over. I hadn't noticed her before, but she's incredibly cute with short brunette hair. Almost like a hip version of the Huntress which, admittedly, is an odd coincidence.

Our paths converged and it was apparent she was going to say something, so I beat her to it. "Sorry about staring. I didn't mean to."

"I get that all the time," she returned coolly. Then she smiled because she was teasing.

I felt a reaction to her response, sort of like I wanted to grin, too, so I chose to move on.

"Oh, my God," she exclaimed, stopping me short.

"What?" I asked.

"You almost smiled!"

It was a lame joke, only I wasn't used to be joked with.

"Who's in charge of the school newspaper?" she asked. "Do you know? I need to go track down a reporter."

17

"Amusing," I replied dryly. "Again, I apologize for staring," I said as I started forward.

"It's okay. You couldn't help it."

"I said I didn't mean to, not that I couldn't help it," I corrected.

She looked like she might burst into laughter. And who could blame her?

As I headed to my next class, it took a few seconds to realize she was trotting along beside me. I kept my gaze on the path in front of me, because that's how you do it when you're invisible. You don't make eye contact. You don't acknowledge anyone or strike up conversation.

"See ya, Matt," she said cheerfully right before I turned into chemistry.

My heart did this weird little flip-flop because, somehow, she knew my name and what class I was going to.

Because we're on the block system, I only have four classes. This semester I have AP World History, Honors Chemistry, Honors Calculus, and AP English. I got stuck with first lunch, which is the last part of block two. Our school is overcrowded, so we have six lunch periods going from 10:55 until 2:10. That day at lunch, I sat in my normal spot, the back table on the right hand side, and pulled out my chemistry homework. I'd downed half my tasteless, generic-brand turkey lunch meat sandwich when I sensed someone hovering over my left shoulder.

"What is the relationship between the order of the reactant and the exponent for the reactant in the rate law?" she read from my textbook.

Of course, I knew who it was since I'd just heard her voice an hour before. I didn't turn around, nor did I need to since she came around the table and plunked down across from me. She was carrying an apple, a bottle of water and a bag of Doritos.

"Do you even know my name?" she asked. "You don't, do you?"

"We've never officially met, so how would I?" I replied, trying to keep my voice neutral. I didn't want to be rude, but we didn't need to act like friends either. I'd made this far without any and I'm pretty close to the finishing line. A little over four months, then the summer, then one more year and then I'm out. So, so out.

"Everybody here knows *something* about everyone else." She took a bite of the apple.

I shrugged. "I don't."

"Except you," she agreed when she'd swallowed. "I'm Graylin, by the way."

She stuck out her hand, so I didn't have a lot of choice. I shook it.

"I know, it's an unusual name," she continued. "You've never heard it before. It's Celtic." She opened the bag of chips and offered me one.

"No, thanks."

"Because you don't like Doritos? Or maybe you like cool ranch but not nacho cheese? Or *maybe* you're afraid that sharing my Doritos would mean you *owe* me."

I had to hand it to her; she could mock with the best of them. I took another bite of my sandwich and then, on impulse, I reached over and took a Dorito. I held it up, studied it and then shoved it into my mouth.

"The boy owes me now," she said under her breath.

"Yeah, you got me," I replied, after I had the good grace to finish the bite. "So what is it you want?"

"*Hmm*. I'd like to know two things," she replied thoughtfully. "One, why were you looking at me the way you were today?"

"I couldn't help it?"

She laughed and I felt it again. That pull. You're standing on the soft wet sand of the shore, the breeze is blowing and the tide is coming in. You just want to step forward and feel the waves tickle your toes.

"C'mon, seriously," she said.

I took a breath but couldn't come up with a single word of explanation.

"Wow, is it that hard?"

19

"Apparently. Maybe we should move on."

"Okay, but I thought the first question was the easy one," she warned.

"Don't you ever stare off in a daze?"

"It's high school," she replied drolly. "Yeah. But you didn't look … dazed."

I shrugged. "Your second question?"

"What's your deal?"

I cocked my head. "What do you mean?"

"What is it with you?" she asked earnestly. "There's all this speculation, but—"

I was confused by the half-uttered statement and also more than a little suspicious that I was being set up for a joke. "What are you talking about?"

"You know."

"*Uhh*, no, I don't."

"That you think you're some sort of a god is the most popular theory." She suddenly jerked with laughter. "Your mouth just dropped open."

I looked around, wondering if an entire lunch table was watching us, ready to burst into obnoxious laughter. Not seeing one, I looked back at her, wondering if she was just messing with me, but now she looked taken aback, which freaked me out even more. "You're kidding," I stammered. "I mean you're …kidding about that. Right? Just messing with me?"

She shook her head and looked almost sad.

She was seriously messing with my head. "Why do you look like that?"

"Because you really didn't know," she said slowly. "You don't think that."

"That I'm a god?" I asked incredulously. All I could do was shake my head. Not like saying no, but like completely blown out of the water. *A god?* What was she talking about? I was *invisible.*

She sat back, took another bite of apple and studied me thoughtfully. "Now, I'm even more intrigued."

I felt trapped in the center of a glaring spotlight and, if it's not obvious by now, I'm not a spotlight kind of guy. "I assure you, there's nothing to be intrigued about."

"Oh, I think there is. You're one of the best-looking guys in the school, highly intelligent, but incredibly aloof. Like off the charts aloof."

Pretty much all I heard was 'one of the best-looking guys in school.' Maybe I was a psychology project for her. How much can you mess with one guy's head in the span of five minutes?

"It's almost like you really don't see the rest of us," she continued.

"Because I don't," I admitted. "Usually."

"How do you do that?"

"It's easy. It's work to get to know people, to get them to accept you. Being invisible is easy."

She made a snorting noise that was totally *un*self conscience and anything but ladylike. "Uhh, sorry to break it to you, friend, but you are most definitely not invisible."

The bell rang, and I had mixed reactions about it, part relief and part regret. Graylin started wolfing Doritos down. She offered me the bag again, but I shook my head. "No way. Those things come with too high a price."

She laughed, spewing a piece of Dorito.

Damn it. The wave crashed over me, and I smiled, too.

21

4

Trance One

Have you ever noticed how when one little thing changes in your life, everything suddenly takes on a slightly different color and tempo? After the Graylin encounter, I found myself looking around, noticing the other kids and wondering how they perceived me. Transitioning from anesthetized to self-aware is a way bigger leap than you might think.

Although I'd resolved not to play any more Ruaun3 for a while, it's alarming how fast the resolution disintegrated once I got home. All I wanted to do was to turn on the computer and launch a game. Instead, trying to stay strong, I got busy. As in hyper-drive busy. Doing laundry, cleaning the apartment, making a grocery list, calculating the amount of funds the groceries would take and leaving a note detailing all it for Mom. On top of that, every few minutes I threw jabs and kicks at an invisible boxing opponent to burn off excess energy.

I thought about getting out of the apartment and running. Instead, I found myself staring into the bathroom mirror trying to see myself objectively. One of the best-looking guys in school? I could not believe she'd said that. I'm just shy of six feet with medium brown hair and hazel eyes. There's nothing unattractive about me, but there's nothing outstanding either.

Maybe just one game, I thought. (I know, I know. The reasoning of an addict.)

I went to my computer and reached out to turn it on, but I didn't. Then I did, but to work on my essay only. That occupied me for half an hour, during which I came up with a total of six sentences, probably none of which I'll keep. I was just too distracted.

Out of curiosity, I googled **hallucination**. According to an online dictionary, a hallucination is defined as perception in the absence of a stimulus. Was that what had happened to me in History? Was I delusional? I'd never thought of myself as delusional. If you're delusional, don't you suspect it on some level?

I meandered from one search to another, segueing from **Delusions** to **mental illness** to **treatments for mental illness** to a half dozen more topics, eventually ending up at **hypnosis**. I almost skipped to the next topic, but something held my attention long enough to read an article and to start wondering if maybe it was legit.

The article said that a person who goes under hypnosis is always in control. Nobody can make you do or say anything. Those TV segments where a hypnotist does their thing and then makes people bark like dogs or act like celebrities is total BS. Hypnosis is actually about using the power of your mind to get control of something in your life.

I like that.

Next, I read about self-hypnosis. I figured it wouldn't work for me, because restlessness would kick in and my attention would wander, but it couldn't hurt to try. Worst-case scenario, I'd waste my time. It just so happens, that's what I do best in life. Besides, maybe I'd figure out the conflict I'd buried so deeply in my subconscious that I was imagining seeing Sirena in real life.

I read the instructions of hypnotizing one's self a couple of times and then mentally tested myself on the steps and passed. Step one is to get comfortable, so I went to my bed, propped up pillows against my headboard and sat back against them, moving them around until they were perfect. Next, I was to breathe slowly, relax and state my goal. "Okay. Umm. My goal is to go into a, uh, trance to … figure out the whole Sirena thing."

Yeah, okay. That part felt kind of stupid.

Next, I was supposed to tell myself how I'm going to feel afterwards. "I'll feel a lot better if I'm not schizoid," I muttered. On second thought, that didn't seem good enough, plus something had been said about establishing the amount of time you were going to spend at it, so I tried again. "In a half hour, I will feel better knowing more about whatever is going on in my head. A half hour," I repeated. "One half hour."

I decided to get to the actual process. The first step was the induction. I was supposed to look around and notice three things one at a time. Go slowly, look at each of them for a moment. Next, I was to pay attention to three sounds, one at a time. Then I was to pay close attention to three physical feelings or sensations. After that, I would close my eyes and picture something, then imagine a sound and then a feeling. After that, I would repeat the process, except with two images, sounds and feelings. Etcetera.

I looked over and noticed a gold plastic cup next to my computer. It used to have a logo on it, but it's worn off. I don't even remember what the logo was. I looked around and my eye caught on the stack of college catalogues on my dresser. One had a bright green spine. I looked down and studied the pattern of white squares on my blue bedspread.

Sounds.

The hum of my computer. The soft bang as the furnace kicked in. A car going by.

Feelings.

The pillows behind me. The pressure of my arms on my legs. Relaxing.

I closed my eyes and breathed slowly. I pictured Graylin offering me her bag of Doritos. I remembered the sound of her biting into her apple. That feeling of giving into a smile.

Two things. I pictured the gold plastic cup and the apple. Graylin's lips beside it.

The *sound* of a clock ticking, the squeal of distant breaks.

The *feeling* of going to sleep, dropping off to sleep.

Three things.

I pictured Sirena on the computer screen and then I remembered Sirena as she'd looked in my dream. I thought of the photograph of Madison Perry getting ready to blow out her birthday candles.

Sounds. The Happy Birthday song being sung. The sound of blowing out candles. Sirena's voice, saying, *And there may be more.*

Feelings. Walking. The feeling of walking.

Except I actually felt myself walking. *So this is it*, I thought, *I'm doing it*. And I was. I was walking down a dimly lit hall next to Sirena. I glanced over at her, but she stared straight ahead. There was a door in front of us, cracked open so that bright light shone from beyond. Sirena's step faltered and she gestured me onward, so I walked past her and pushed open the door.

For a second, the light was so bright, I couldn't see anything, but then I found myself outside in the middle of a wide-open space on a spring day. Madison Perry was walking toward me with a smile on her lips. A breeze blew a strand of hair in her face and she brushed it back. Then I saw Kaci Smith swinging on a swing, one of an old two-swing variety with a teeter-tooter and a slide. The fading red and white striped poles had obviously been painted by hand and not very well.

Ellyn Lamb sat at the base of the slide with her ankles crossed. She watched me, frowning pensively, as if trying to decide whether to say something or not. "She shouldn't come," she said to me. "She shouldn't be here."

I thought she was referring to Madison and so I drew breath to tell her it was too late, Madison was already there, but then I saw a girl who couldn't have been more than nine or ten years old running toward the swing set from another direction.

Stop her, Sirena commanded from behind. She hadn't said it. She'd thought it, but somehow I'd gotten the message. I raised my hand to stop the girl, right as the dryer in our apartment buzzed.

I gasped and my eyes flew open. My heart pounded painfully. I scooted off the bed, breathing hard and trying to make sense of what I'd just experienced, but my knees were so weak that I had to sit back down again. The memory of the trance was painfully clear, but I didn't have a clue as to what it meant.

25

5

Mealtime Convo

Graylin wasn't in first block the next morning, which was a disappointment. Then the fact that it was a disappointment was a disappointment because I really didn't need to start depending on anyone at this juncture. We had a pop quiz, designed to scare everyone straight into studying for the upcoming test. *Whatever.* I aced it.

At lunch, I doodled as I tried coming up with ideas for my college application essay, but my mind kept going back to the trance I'd experienced. I puzzled over what each thing could have meant, but not only was I short on answers, I was short on possibilities. Was it possible that the mind churned up stuff in trances the way it does in dreams? If so, maybe it was just stress and some unresolved conflict taking the form of unexpected people and places and situations. Maybe none of it meant anything.

A bag of Cool Ranch Doritos dropped in front of me, and I felt a moment of elation. Graylin walked around and stationed herself in front of me with a wrapped sandwich and a Diet Pepsi in hand. I'd already scarfed down my generic-brand PB and J. "I like Natcho Cheese better," I said, opening the bag.

"Duly noted," she replied. She opened the plastic wrap around her sandwich. The smell of tuna fish hit me, which wasn't a problem, I like tuna fish. "The question is," she said in an ominous tone. "Do you have the nerve to eat those? Well, half of them, because I want some."

I crunched into one and waggled my eyebrows, and she chuckled. "Where were you in first?" I asked.

She made a slurpy sound with her mouth. "Slept in. Oops."

"You missed a quiz."

She rolled her eyes. "That class is worthless. Some teachers, who shall remain nameless, should have retired fifteen years ago if they should have ever gone into teaching in the first place, which I have profound doubts about."

I nodded because I did not disagree.

She took a bite of her sandwich. "So, tell me more."

"About the quiz?"

She curled her lip. "Would I threaten your honor? I meant more about you, of course."

I shrugged. "There's not much to tell."

"Oh, c'mon, entertain me. It's not like you have something better to do right now than to talk to me."

"I go to school and back home again. I work part time at Hannah's Hardware. It's this family-owned business a couple of blocks from us."

"Do you like it?"

"I do."

"You're a junior, right?"

I nodded. "Although I've been told I'm wise for my age."

She grinned. "Thought about college yet? Where you want to go?"

"Cambridge," I replied without hesitation.

She gave me a look. "As in the UK?"

"You asked where I *wanted* to go. I'll end up going somewhere in state. Tuition and all."

"Cambridge would be cool, though, wouldn't it?"

"Oh, yeah. Maybe in my next lifetime when I come back as filthy rich." She opened the soda, and I made a mental note of the sound. I was storing up sounds and images today.

"I think I'll be a rock star next time," she said.

"Can you sing?"

She grimaced and shook her head. "God, no. When I start singing in the shower, the soap melts just so it can get out of there faster."

I laughed because she was so wacky and so totally comfortable with it. I admired that.

28

"You look good when you smile," she commented. "You should do it more often."

"Duly noted."

"So, what do you want to study at Cambridge … or wherever?"

"I don't know. I like math and history and I kind of like the idea of teaching. At a college level. Or maybe something to do with psychology. Figuring people out is interesting. At the moment, my only subject is me, which is pretty boring." Okay, that wasn't entirely true, but I sure wasn't going there. "What about you?"

"What do I want to be when I grow up?" she asked looking strangely entertained.

A loud squeak of a chair across the cafeteria rudely interrupted our flow of conversation, followed by a guy yelling, "Get out of my face, freaks!"

It was another altercation between the mourners and stoners I'd seen the day before. One girl was crying, and the stoners were laughing. "What's their problem?" I asked testily.

"Dora and her group are just messing," Graylin replied, her tone full of disgust.

"Is Dora skunk girl?"

The corners of her mouth quirked. "Fitting name."

I looked back over at the table and the guy, the jock, was leaning on the stoners table saying something, directing it to Dora. He was pissed. She, however, looked to be thoroughly enjoying herself. "Why are they messing with them?"

"Because they're seriously screwed up. Dora Blake is the leader and she's only a freshman. A real little psychopath in the making."

The stoners got up to leave, still chuckling from whatever joke they'd shared. They took their good, sweet time filing out and then, at the door, Dora turned back and gave the jock a flirty little wave, right before she flipped her hand around and flew him the bird. In that moment, her expression went cold as ice. Cold as pure hate.

"I bet her mother is proud," I said as Dora exited through the double doors, slamming them back as hard as she could.

"Her mother abdicated a long time ago. Dora lives in a group home."

Wow. Graylin really did know something about everyone, it seemed. "Abdicated," I repeated, looking at Graylin. "Good word. I think I'm turned on."

"Oh, I know lots of big words," she said in a cartoon voice.

I grinned and glanced back over at the jock's lunch table. "Is that guy Madison Perry's boyfriend or something?"

"*Uhh*, no. That's Ty Larkin, the football player. You know, *Ty Larkin*. You hear his name the whole season. The whole year. Ty Larkin?" she repeated, just in case I hadn't heard the first two times.

I shrugged. "I don't follow school sports that closely."

"See the girl sitting next to him, the one crying? That's Nikki. That's his girlfriend. She and Madison were good friends. They cheered together. Madison made the varsity team as a freshman, which never happens."

"Do you know this much about most the kids here?"

"Pretty much. Ty can be a loudmouth, especially when he's pissed, but he's a good guy. Which is the only reason Dora's four are messing with them. Because they can see it get to them."

"Dora's four. Sounds like a children's program."

"It is so anything but," she replied darkly before she helped herself to some Doritos. "So, you want to hang out sometime?"

My mouth went dry. "Sure, but I ... don't have a car."

She shrugged. "I do."

"Yeah. Okay. Sure. Yeah, I definitely do. That would be great." I finally stopped myself from speaking further. What can I say? Sometimes the brain freezes and the mouth just keeps going. The brain is aware of it, an inner consciousness already growing alarmed if not horrified, but still, the mouth goes on.

She fished into her pocket and came out with a sticky note with her name and number written on it. "My card, sir."

It said **Graylin Hall. 758-1446.**

"Hall," I said, because I hadn't known her last name.

"Matthews," she returned. "Your name sounds like a news guy to me. 'And now your local sportscast with Matt Matthews,'" she said in a phony announcer voice.

I grinned. "What about Graylin Hall?"

Her expression turned mournful. "Sounds like a college dorm. Where you living at?" she asked in a goofy voice. "I'm in Graylin Hall." Her expression suddenly changed. "Oooh. That sounded kind of sexual, didn't it?"

"Not touching it," I replied, throwing my hands in the air. I felt some heat in my face and hoped it wasn't obvious. Guys are not supposed to blush. It's just fundamentally wrong.

"I dig that self-restraint," she said, seemingly oblivious to my discomfort. She reached for another Dorito. "My sister's name is Haley. I always say 'Hidy ho, Haley Hall.'" Graylin wrinkled her nose. "She loves that."

She is so out there, which I totally envy. The bell rang, and I watched her scarf down the rest of her sandwich, taking huge bites. "I know, I know," she muttered, barely understandable because her mouth was full and her hand covering it to spare me the gory details. "My mother would be so proud."

~~~

I was finishing up my calculus homework that evening when the mouthwatering scent of sizzling beef caught my attention. It could mean only one thing. The planets had aligned just so, resulting in my mom cooking. Let's just say *not* a frequent occurrence in my world. I bounded downstairs, ravenous with hunger, and rejoiced to behold hamburger patties being fried. There was a pan of mac and cheese on the stove and a can of name brand baby peas on the counter. I'm telling you, it was a thing of beauty. I picked up the can of peas and gave her a critical look. "You paid more for these."

She smiled a cockeyed smile. "Call it crazy living on my part." She looked up from the pan of mac and cheese she was studiously stirring and shrugged. "They were on sale, anyway."

31

I took a sip of her wine and then moved the glass over to get to the can opener so I could open the peas. "I had lunch with this girl today."

Mom gave me a *whoo-hoo* look.

"She said my name reminded her of a sports guy on TV."

Mom reached for her wine and took a drink. "I always thought it was a cool name. One you don't forget."

"I always thought it was totally idiotic to have the same first and last name."

She looked astonished. "Really?" she exclaimed, her voice dripping with sarcasm. "Cause I don't think you've ever mentioned that."

I drained the peas, poured them in a bowl, covered it with plastic wrap and stuck it in the microwave. "This'll only take a minute or two. We ready?"

"Go for it. By the way, you got some more crap from colleges."

I looked over and saw three new look books. I usually check the mail, but I'd been distracted that afternoon.

"I don't know how we're going to afford it," she muttered.

It's what she always said. And I always had the same reply. "Financial aid."

"I don't know how any of that works."

I almost groaned because it was the same conversation over and over. I could actually say both our parts word for word. "We'll figure it out."

"You want milk or water?"

"Milk."

"So, get it."

I shook my head as I went for the milk. It's not that I'm used to being served but, as already stated, I'm not used to her cooking either. We sat and began eating, and it was good. There really is something to be said for eating real food at a real table with real company. I'm a fan.

"So what's your favorite so far?" she asked.

I looked up sharply. "My favorite?"

"College." She smirked. "What were *you* thinking about?"

"Nothing."

"Then why you turning red? What's her name, anyway?"

"Who?" I asked, playing innocent.

She crossed her eyes. "Oh, what? You have lunch with a new girl every day? They take a number or something? See who the lucky one is?"

"That is exactly what happens. Girls line up each and every morning and—"

"So, what's her name?"

"Graylin."

"Now *that's* a weird name."

"One you don't forget," I said.

"You going to ask her out?"

"We'll probably hang out."

"Oh, is that what we call it now? Just make sure you're not *hanging* out enough to get her pregnant."

I made a sound of disgust. "Come on. Just because—"

"Uh-uh-uh. Don't go there," she warned.

"I'm not stupid enough to get anyone pregnant. Okay?"

"Good. Because I am so not ready to be a grandma."

I almost asked if she was about ready to be a mother but restrained myself. What would be the point, anyway? "For whatever it counts, I like this," I said, waving my fork over the plate. "Why don't we do this every night?"

"Tell you what, when Chef Boyardee becomes available and can move into our servant's quarters, we'll do this every night."

"Then once a week. Why can't we do this once a week?"

"What are you talking about?" she asked irritably. "We do."

I opened my mouth to refute the statement, but, *again*, what would the point be? Besides, she was looking kind of ashamed all the sudden. Very not like her.

"I was thinking maybe we'd have spaghetti next week," she said, keeping her eyes on her plate.

My comment *had* gotten to her. "That would be great," I replied. "And I'm hoping for Davidson."

33

She looked up, confused.

"College," I said. "You asked what my favorite was so far. It's hard to get in, but I'm hoping.

"They expensive?"

"Financial aid, mom. We should be fine. I don't think it will cost you a dime."

"I don't mind if it costs me a dime. That's about what I got."

I couldn't help it; a groan escaped me.

After the kitchen was cleaned up, I went back upstairs, finished calc and tried another self-hypnosis session. For an hour, I relaxed, followed the mental exercises and got absolutely zero results. Now I'm wondering if last time I got so relaxed that I actually went to sleep. I *thought* I'd worked myself into a trance, but maybe it was just a crazy dream. I wish I could really convince myself that was the case, forget about it and just move on.

6

Hoops

A North Carolina February can be below freezing one day and then hit fifty degrees with sunshine the next. That Saturday, as I walked to work, that's where the temperature was headed. It was a nice change.

The yellow and maroon façade of Hannah's Hardware was in sight when my cell phone rang. It's embarrassing to admit, but it actually startled me. *Probably a wrong number*, I thought as I pulled it from my jacket pocket, but the phone showed it was Graylin since I'd already stored her number. I came to a dead stop. "Hello?"

"Hey. It's Graylin," she said. It sounded like her mouth was full.

"Hey."

"Sorry. I'm eating a bagel."

"Oh." (Yeah, I know. What a sparkling conversationalist I can be.) "I'm just going into work."

"You want to shoot some hoops later?"

"Uhh, yeah."

"What time do you get off?"

"Five o'clock, but I could see if I could get off early."

"It's open gym day because the team has an away game. No one ever goes, but—"

"No, I'd love to. What time?"

"It's open until eight, so you don't have to get off early."

"Okay. How 'bout if I meet you at, like, five thirty?"

"I'll be there, all sexy looking in my boy shorts and baggy t."

I laughed. "Basketball's not really my game, but—"

"Great! I'm in the mood to kick someone's ass today. So, I'm just going to go ahead and scratch that one off my list knowing we'll get to it later."

"Okay, then," I returned cheerfully.

"Later, dude," she chirped.

I couldn't stop grinning as I continued on my way. If I'd had a tenth of Graylin Hall's confidence, I would have kicked up my heels and danced the mambo into work and not given a damn what anyone thought.

Hannah's Hardware is a family business that a man named Everett Hannah started back in 1892. It passed to his son, Everett Hannah Junior, who passed it to his son, Everett the third, who passed it the current Mr. Hannah. Guess what his name is?

Everett Hannah the fourth, my boss, Ev for short, has two sons. The eldest, Everett Hannah the fifth, although everyone calls him Rhett, doesn't work at the store much anymore since he's in his third year of college. He's getting a degree in archeology, which Ev gets a real kick out of. "So he can come back here and dig through the inventory," he often jokes. Toby, their younger son, is nineteen and has Down syndrome. He's kind to everybody, doesn't have mean bone in his body, but, occasionally, punks make fun of him. That's the only time I ever want to get violent.

That day, time flew. Afterwards, I ran home, changed and ran to the gym, half expecting Graylin not to be there. I heard the sound of balls bouncing as I made way to the gym. I passed a security guard who nodded at me. "Hey," I said. My heart was beating fast as I opened one of the double doors. I walked in, trying to seem all cool and low key as I looked around at the maybe fifteen kids there. I didn't see Graylin.

"Yo, Matthews," she called.

Oh, the relief I felt. The happiness. I looked over at her just in time to catch the basketball she'd thrown. "Oh! So, it's going to be like that?" I threw it back. "Mind if I take my coat off first?"

"No, go ahead," she said. Then she faked a pass, making me pause. "Oh, come on. I wouldn't do that. Really. Go on."

I could see how this was going to go. I turned my back, slipped off my coat, tossed it onto the bleachers and then turned and ran at her. It was on, and it was fun. We played a little one on one and three games of Horse. She's pretty good, but I only had to nay once, and only because of a stupid backwards, over the head shot she's gotten down to a science. Afterwards, we sat on the bleachers and watched others playing. Mostly they were goofing, but one girl was really good.

"It's kind of surprising the gym is open," I said, watching the girl make a half-court shot. "I mean, this soon after—"

Graylin nodded. "They're trying to keep things normal. We children need normalcy, you know."

"Normalcy, huh?"

"Yeah. You know the place?"

"Can't say that I do. I spend much of my life on another planet."

"Oh, yeah? Which one? Mars, like every other guy in the world?"

"Nope. Ruaun3."

She grinned and elbowed me. "I *love* that game. I play as Smoke. She rules!"

"I agree."

"What level are you?"

"Five."

"Of the newest version?"

"Yep."

"Shut up. Really? Level five?"

"Cross my heart."

"I can't get beyond four. I may have to get some tips from you."

I picked up the ball and spun it on my finger for a few seconds. "Might cost you."

"Like what? The magic two questions?"

I leaned on the ball. "Just one actually. Same one you asked me. What's the deal with you?"

She looked mystified and then shook her head. "Expound."

"You fascinate me. You're like one of the sea birds on the coast that float above everything. Not fly but just kind of float in the wind."

Any trace of a smile had vanished from her face.

"I mean it is a good thing," I added quickly. "I'm envious. You just seem miles above all of us."

"I'm right here."

Now she seemed either worried or defensive or something. I hadn't meant to do that. "I know but somehow you're not mired in the muck. It's like you've got it figured out."

"I wish I did." She stood. "Let's hit it. Can I drop you at home?"

"Nah," I said, handing her the ball. "My mom's coming soon."

"Then I'll wait with you."

"No, go. I'll catch you later."

"You sure?"

I nodded. "This was fun."

She reached for her coat and tossed it over her shoulder. "It was. Later."

"See ya."

After she left, I pondered every word I'd said. Somehow, I seemed to have sapped the ease between us and part of her composure. Why? I'd meant what I said is a compliment. That's how I thought of it. I watched the game in progress for a couple of minutes and then slipped out and walked home afraid that maybe I'd screwed things up.

7

Bizarreville

Minutes after the dismissal bell rang the following Monday, I stood at the front doors and stared out dejectedly at a pelting rain. Everyone else shot past me, anxious to be free of school. I did not feel the same optimism. Not only was it just above freezing and pouring, but Graylin hadn't been at school again. After a taste of the buddy thing, going back to being my lone, pathetic self sucked.

"Matt?" a girl called from behind me.

I turned, half expecting there to be another Matt in the vicinity and saw two girls approaching – and they were looking at me.

"Hey," one greeted with a friendly smile.

"Hey," I returned.

"You ready for the calc test tomorrow?"

Oh, yeah. I had seen her in calculus. *Taylor*, I thought. I shrugged and concentrated on not blushing. "Think so."

"I don't suppose you'd want to come join our study group?" she asked hopefully.

I barely stopped my jaw from dropping.

"It would be so great if you could," the other girl spoke up. "I mean, you always seem to get it."

I had no idea who she was. "*Uh—*"

"We're getting pizza," Taylor added as an enticement. As if.

"Oh, you mean … today?" I stammered.

She made a face as if she was in physical pain. "Too short notice?"

"I don't have my car," I said choppily. (And, by the way, technically speaking, that's true. Misleading, perhaps, but true.)

"That's no problem," Taylor said. "I'll drop you off later. It would *so* be great if you could."

"Please," the other girl wheedled.

"Sure, I guess I could." *Weird.* The voice that had spoken sounded a lot like mine. I would have been surer about it except for that I was having some sort of out-of-body experience.

They both beamed, which was nice.

"Do you know Steph?" Taylor asked.

Steph laughed and rolled her eyes. "Obviously we've *seen* each other."

I nodded and smiled back, although I swear, I had never seen her before.

"And, of course, you know Morgan," Steph said, gesturing to Taylor, who apparently is Morgan.

"Yeah," I lied. I mean, what was I going to say?

"Look at the rain," Morgan whined as she looked beyond me. "I didn't bring an umbrella or anything."

I looked back outside just as an old-style black Camaro pulled up and honked, its music blaring loudly enough to vibrate the building.

"Yes," Morgan exclaimed. "Come on," she said to me before she dashed outside.

The guy in the car leaned over to unlock the passenger side door, and it was the jock I'd noticed being harassed by the skunk club. So I was joining Ty Larkin, football star of NHS, and his friends? Unless I was immediately frozen out as soon as I got into the car, which is probably what would happen.

"Come on," Steph urged.

I honestly don't know the words to convey how out of place I felt as I followed her out the door and into the backseat of the car. Morgan was holding the door open for us, meaning she'd called shotgun.

Ty turned down the music. "Hey," he greeted me with a friendly salute like wave.

"Do you know Matt?" Morgan asked Ty.

"Seen him around," Ty replied. He looked at me through the rear-view mirror. "You good at calculus?"

"I get it, pretty much."

"That makes one of us. You want me to take you to your car now or bring you back later?" he asked Morgan.

"Later. Hopefully it'll stop raining by then."

Ty put the car into gear and drove. So I wasn't being immediately frozen out. I was actually going with them. And there were no fireworks in sight.

"I love this song," Morgan exclaimed before cranking the radio back up.

It was surreal to be driving down the road with these guys, jamming to Rihanna. So perfectly normal for most people, but not me. A commercial came on and Ty turned down the radio again.

"Nikki's rubbed off on you," Morgan said disparagingly.

"Remind me to tell her you said that."

"So. Matt," Steph said, shifting to face me. "What do you do when you're not at school?"

"I work."

"Oh, yeah? Where?"

"Hannah's Hardware."

"I always thought that was a weird name for a hardware store," Ty remarked. "Was it named after a girl named Hannah?"

"No, Hannah's their last name."

"Wait a sec," Ty said. "Rhett Hannah?"

"Yeah, he's the oldest son."

Ty nodded. "Cool guy. Hell of a high jumper."

"He is a good guy," I agreed.

"And his little brother is, *uhh*—"

"He has Down syndrome," I supplied.

"I remember that," Ty said.

"Toby," I added. "He's like the kindest person on the face of the earth. Always positive." I don't know why I felt the need to say this, except, occasionally, if anyone mentions someone with a mental disability, somebody else in the vicinity feels the need to do a parody, which pisses me off.

"Yeah, Rhett was great with him," Ty said. "You know? Proud. Or maybe proud's not the word. But he'd wave at him at meets and stuff. I always thought it was cool."

"I know what you mean," Steph spoke up. "He wasn't going to act all ashamed."

"Yeah. It's like, screw it, that's my brother. You don't like it? Get the fuck over it."

I was relieved by the tone of the conversation. "They're close," I said. "Rhett calls him every Sunday and tells him about his week. Although, I'm pretty sure he gives the censored version."

Ty chuckled and glanced back at me in the rearview mirror. When he pulled into his driveway and under a carport, I realized the Larkin home is only six or eight streets over from our apartment. What a difference a few blocks can make. They weren't mansions or anything. They're middle income, well-maintained homes with trees in the yards, sidewalks along the streets and basketball hoops on garages. I would have so happily lived there.

Everyone piled out of the car. Another car was parked on the street with two people inside. One was Ty's girlfriend, or so Graylin had informed me. Nikki. "Got the pizza," she called as she popped out of the car. Her coat had a hood, which she'd pulled up. Hunched over, she ran to join us, as did another guy.

I stayed in back of the group, feeling way out of place. At least I didn't have that far to walk home if it got too uncomfortable.

"Hello," Nikki greeted me with a friendly smile. She tossed her hood back and I saw she was prettier than I'd realized.

"This is Nikki," Steph introduced. "And Mike."

Mike gave that quick uplift of the head that jocks do. I wasn't about to try pulling it off because I'd look like a poser. "Hey," I said instead.

Ty unlocked the door and we all went into a homey kitchen that is exactly what kitchens are supposed to look like. There's a pot rack above a center island loaded with copper pots and pans, there's an impressively filled wine rack that would take my mom at least a couple of very happy weeks to work through, and there was a basket of fresh fruit and a big Tupperware container of muffins. It was the kind of place the family sits down to dinner every night and talks about their day. Meanwhile, eight blocks over, I'm heating up canned ravioli and hoping the store brand milk hasn't soured.

"Let's eat," Ty roared. He opened the fridge and pulled out a six-pack of Coke, the real thing, not a generic, and set it on the counter.

Pizza boxes were opened and, for once, my stomach didn't churn at the smell. It was better quality than Mom usually gets.

"There's left-over fried chicken, too, if anyone wants it," Ty said, sticking it out on the counter.

Oh, to live like this. Ty opened the Tupperware lid that covered the chicken and my mouth literally watered from the aroma. Oh, yeah. I wanted it. I wanted it so much, I may have been trembling in my restraint not to pounce and shove it into my face. Nikki was in a cabinet pulling out chips and cookies. She appeared to feel pretty much at home in the Larkin residence.

The next ten or fifteen minutes were an eating and talking frenzy. I chowed on chicken and salty, name brand chips and even a slice of supreme pizza, which actually lived up to its name. As to the conversation, I listened, feeling like a visitor from another planet while trying not to look like it. I didn't know anyone they were talking about. There were some catchy names like, Suzy Slut; I'm guessing that was a nickname, and Hunter Hultberg. I have no idea if that was a nickname or not. If not, it's a name that would be difficult to enunciate if one was highly inebriated. That's what I was thinking when Mike asked me if I played any sports.

"Not really," I replied, hating that the attention had shifted to me. I felt like I'd magically slipped through the cracks, but now they'd notice I was there and start to question it. At least, I'd had a chance to eat like a king. "I run and I used to play soccer."

"You should go for the team," Ty spoke up. "More than half the starters graduated last year."

"Yeah, but they've still got talent," Mike interjected. "Fields, O'neal, Gary Jones."

"More ego than talent in my opinion," Ty said.

"Ty," Nikki chastised. "You shouldn't say that."

Nikki had darkened circles under her eyes.

"Nik, how many times I gotta tell you? I'm not Mother Teresa."

"I play soccer," Steph said, directing it to me.

I nodded politely and felt totally conspicuous.

"I have a terrible feeling I'm going to bomb this calculus test," Nikki said.

"You always say that," Morgan said, rolling her eyes. "And you never do."

"Nope, Nik's right," Ty said. "Let's get started."

There was a general exodus and some of the food was hauled into a family room as nice and comfortable as the kitchen. Everybody found a spot, settled in and opened their calculus books and notebooks, except me. I hadn't brought anything of it.

"Okay," Nikki said. "Here's the first one I couldn't get. The population of a large city can be modeled by $y=1.8e\,0.026\,t$, where $t=0$ corresponds to 1990. In what year is the population of this city expected to reach 2.5 million?" She looked at Ty, sitting next to her, but he looked back at her as if the question had been spoken in an obscure Scandinavian dialect. She looked over at me.

"Um, well, you want to set the population to the formula," I said. "You're trying to find the year."

"So you'd divide the 2.5 million divided by the 1.8, leaving the other side as $e\,0.026t$. Right?"

"Right. Then remember whenever e is raised to a power, you have to take the natural log of both sides." Everybody was writing and figuring. "And the next rule would be to apply the inverse property and simplify."

"What are you, man?" Mike asked me. "Some kind of genius?"

"Hardly."

"I swear, you just made that a thousand times easier than Reynolds ever did," Morgan commented. "You know what I heard?" she asked with a wicked half-smile, flicking her gaze around the group. "I heard he was having a thing with Callie Adams."

"I heard that too," Mike said. "I heard they were in a car making out after school one day."

"Sounds like bullshit to me," Ty commented. "I mean, why would a teacher be so stupid? You'd get fired if anyone saw you."

"Hey, it happens," Mike said.

"So, Matt," Nikki said, totally ignoring the banter. "After taking the natural logs of both sides, you're left with t=12.6 years?"

I got the impression that she didn't like gossip. She'd all but said so when the subject of Suzy Slut came up and then she'd said something when Ty made a comment about the guys on the soccer team. "Yeah. Now just put 12.6 in the place of e and you get your answer."

Nikki heaved a sigh of relief and smiled.

"I got it, too," Steph said jubilantly.

Mike leaned closer to look at her paper. "I don't get it."

In a low voice, she began explaining the problem again.

"So, Matthews," Ty said.

It surprised me for a second that he really did know my name. No one had called me anything other than Matt that afternoon.

"Remind me how you find the circumference of an ellipse?" he asked.

His notebook should have weighed more given all the layers of ink that had amassed marking through problems, scribbling explanations and then striking through most of those. He'd also written *I don't get this shit, I hate Calc* and *calculus sucks* a lot. I reminded him and he worked a couple of problems until he got it, at which time he turned to Nikki, gloating with success. "Celebration time," he sang in a bad, falsetto voice.

She grinned and leaned over for a kiss. Luckily, they didn't get all sloppy about it.

"Is there more soda?" Steph asked Ty.

"Yeah," Ty replied. "Help yourself."

She got up and, for some reason, I looked over at her at the most perfectly wrong second, just as she tipped her head sideways in a silent request for me to come with her. She's cute, really cute, with shoulder length hair cut in a lot of different layers, but I experienced this curious feeling of dread. Still, there wasn't a lot of choice, so I got up and followed her. In the kitchen, she pulled out another six-pack from the refrigerator and offered me a Coke.

"No, I'm good. I still have some."

"So, are you seeing anybody?" she asked.

Wow. The direct approach. "Sort of," I hedged. I pictured Sirena so I wouldn't look like I was lying out my teeth. I mean, Steph is cute and all, but I didn't know if I wanted to hang out with her. Plus, the whole no car thing is a serious embarrassment.

"Sort of?"

"I was seeing somebody, but we thought we should take some time, so—"

"Oh. Well, if you want to hang out sometime—"

She left the rest of it hanging, which I was glad for. "Okay."

"I'm really glad you came today."

"Yeah. Me, too."

She smiled and took her soda back into the other room but left the rest of the six-pack out. I lingered a minute and then put the other sodas back in the refrigerator. I don't want to be over-dramatic or anything, but, in being there, it felt like my life had taken an unexpected twist and I needed a second to adjust. I shut the refrigerator door and noticed one of the photographs on the front of it. It froze me. Literally. Like a statue.

There are at least a dozen photographs held up by colorful magnets, but this one was a photograph of the little girl from my trance. The one with the three dead girls. The one who wasn't supposed to be among the dead girls. I looked at the other photographs on the fridge and, sure enough, she was in more of them. And then the back door opened, and *that* girl walked in with her mother. I felt like I'd been caught robbing the place.

Ty walked in from the family room and all of them started talking at once. Ty moved around me to get a mini bottle of apple juice from the refrigerator, the little girl was talking a mile a minute about her soccer game, and the mother smiled and said hi to me.

"Hello," I managed, relieved to still have control over my voice.

"This is Matt," Ty said. "My mom," he said to me. "Tina."

"Nice to meet you, Matt. You guys studying for your calculus test?"

"Yes, ma'am," I replied.

"Calculus sucks," Ty commented. "But Matt gets it."

"Did you hear me," the girl demanded of Ty. "I almost scored a goal."

"Almost, huh?" he said. "Remind me, how many points do you get for almost?"

"Matt, this is Charlie," Mrs. Larkin said.

The girl smiled shyly at me. "Hi."

"It's Charlotte, actually," Ty said.

Charlie's smile instantly vanished. "Shut up Tyrone," she says dragging the last part of the name out.

He laughed. "Except my name's really Ty," he said to me, "so she can't get back at me."

"I can tell everyone it's Tyrone," she threatened.

"Whatever. I can prove it's not."

Tina Larkin smiled and rolled her eyes, as if we were sharing a joke. She's older than my mom, but a pretty lady. Classy. "Do you have brothers or sisters, Matt?"

"No, ma'am."

47

"Did you hear that, Ty? *'Ma'am.'* I love that." She reached over and patted my shoulder. "You can come over anytime, Matt."

"Yeah, well, I'll talk to him about that ma'am thing," Ty replied wryly. He looked at me and shook his head. "Sets a bad example, man."

"Sorry, it slipped out," I said, feeling slightly less weirded out, since nobody had seemed to notice I was weirded out.

"Don't listen to him, Matt," Tina laughed as she left the room.

Charlie followed her mom, sending her brother one last dirty look.

"Bye, Charlotte," Ty called.

"Bye, Tyrone."

Whoa. I felt like I'd been drop-kicked. I'd been shown Charlie in a trance, obviously as some kind of a warning and then put into a situation where I'd actually met her. Obviously, I had to do something, but what? "You must worry about her," I said to Ty.

"Who?"

"Your little sister. With all that's happened."

"Nah. Whoever the freak is, he's not after little girls." He looked over at a picture on the fridge. "Did you know her?"

I knew he was talking about Madison even before I looked at the picture of four of them taken at a formal dance. Ty, Nikki, Madison and some other guy. "No," I said quietly.

"She was something," he said. "Nobody didn't like her. You know? She was sweet to everyone. Always saw the bright side." He looked at the picture with a wistful expression. "It's so weird. It's only been a week, but it's like everything is different. In a way, we're all just going through this bogus motion. You know?"

I didn't exactly, but I nodded anyway.

"Especially Nik. She has nightmares. Cries all the time. Do you know, she's such a goody two shoes that she had a perfect attendance record until what happened. Not perfect attendance record for the year, I mean since kindergarten. Crazy, huh?"

"That's impressive."

"Everyday I see like this shadow in her eyes. It's really messing with her."

"It'll get better with time," I ventured lamely. What else was I going to say?

"Yeah. Although … I don't think it's the kind of thing you ever get over completely. You know?"

I suddenly felt really claustrophobic. "So, I've got to head out," I said apologetically. "Think you've got it now?"

"Calculus? Hell, no. But it doesn't really matter. Even if I fail the test, I'll still pass the class. So, whatever. If there's anything we've learned in the last week, it's don't sweat the small stuff. You know?" He took his juice and went toward the family room. "Grab your stuff and I'll take you back to your car."

"Oh, I, uh, don't live far."

Ty turned back to me, confused. "Huh?"

"I didn't drive to school." It is so embarrassing being the only one in the world without a freaking car. "My car is—"

"What?"

I wasn't going to come right out and lie. "I don't have one right now."

"That sucks," he commiserated, but not in a shocked or disgusted or superior sort of way. "So, I'll drive you home."

"That's okay," I said. "I don't live far at all."

"Matthews! Shut up already. Get your books and shit."

His mother walked back into the kitchen. "Ty," she said, frowning. "Watch the language."

"Yes, ma'am," he returned with mocking politeness.

She grimaced. "Doesn't sound quite believable from you yet. But keep working it."

"Yes, ma'am," he said. "I'll certainly do that, ma'am."

Tina just shook her head and looked at me. "Are you leaving already?"

"I have to," I replied.

"Well, come back. I can't remember the last time I heard 'ma'am' out of Ty's mouth."

"Wow, Mom," Ty said. "We may be talking Alzheimer's the because I just said it like two seconds ago."

"Funny," she replied drolly.

I followed Ty back into the living room to get my book bag, but suddenly, all I saw was the window leading to the backyard. I had to look. I had to know if the swing set from my dream was there. "Still raining?" I muttered as I walked over and looked.

Oh, man.

There it was. Just like I'd seen it. The rain had stopped for the moment, but the wind had apparently kicked up, because the swings moved slightly. The sight of it gave me the heebie-jeebies.

"Matthews is bailing," Ty announced.

"Do you really have to?" Morgan whined.

I turned back around to face them. "Yeah. Sorry."

"Matt, thank you so much," Nikki said. "Seriously."

"No problem. You guys call if you get stuck on something."

"What's your number?" Steph asked quickly.

I gave it and she punched it into her phone. Great.

"Matthew's homework hotline," Mike said. "You ought to, like, charge a dollar a call or something. I would."

"Yeah, you would," Morgan agreed.

"I'm going to run him home," Ty said.

"Later, dude," Mike said to me.

"Bye, Matt," Steph said.

"See you guys," I said, and it almost sounded natural. Almost.

As I left the Larkin home, I couldn't help thinking about the movie *Pleasantville*, where Toby McGuire and Reese Witherspoon get sucked into 1950 TV-land. For the past hour, up until seeing Charlie's picture, it had felt a little like I'd been sucked into a modern-day version. But seeing Charlie had changed everything. Now, we were talking Bizarreville, which is just slightly southeast of the twilight zone.

Ty drove me home, which took all of about three minutes. "Thanks, man," we both said at the same time. We laughed. "Call if you need help with anything," I said, reaching for the doorknob.

"Will do. See ya."

Once I was back in the apartment, I felt trapped within the walls. Everything was too quiet. Charlie was real and somehow, I had to protect her. But how? I thought about going for a run, but it was still freezing and drizzling. The thought of talking to Graylin had appeal. If there was anyone who would allow me to get the experience off my chest and not be totally freaked out by it, it would be her. I hoped. Or maybe I could tell her some of it, but not everything. Before I could talk myself out of it, I called her, pacing even faster. When she picked up, I stopped. It's highly possible I'd been hoping for her voice mail to pick up. "Hey, it's Matt."

"I know," she replied sunnily. "Caller ID. What's up?"

Why hadn't I planned out what to say? "Where were you today?"

"Sometimes my social calendar is so full, I just can't fit school in. Did I miss anything important?"

"No."

"I didn't think so."

I started pacing again. I was having second thoughts. If I told her, would she want anything more to do with me? If I didn't, would I go crazy? I sat on our embarrassingly worn couch. "If I tell you something, will you promise not to tell anyone?"

"Unless you tell me you're going to do something drastic or illegal, yes."

"I'm not really the type for that, but you have to swear."

"Okay. I've got three fingers pointing straight up in the air."

"What?"

"Girl scout's honor. Never mind. If this is a personal thing you want to share, I solemnly swear that I will never tell another living soul."

I hesitated. "It's about the dead girls."

Silence. "Then," she finally said, "I don't see how that can possibly be a personal thing, but okay. What about them?"

"This is going to sound crazy, but I had a ... dream about them."

"That's not crazy at all. They're in the news. It's terrible and traumatic. One of them was from North. I mean, you can't help thinking about it. None of us can."

I took a deep breath and exhaled. "Just trust that I'm not completely out of my mind."

"Okay."

"In this dream ... which wasn't like a dream at all, I saw the girls, the victims, all three of them. They were alive in the dream. They were hanging around an old-fashioned swing set. And then I saw someone else, this other little girl that I'd never seen before." She was like nine or ten years old." I paused, but Graylin didn't interject. I almost wanted her to. "Then Ellyn Lamb spoke up and said that she shouldn't be here, meaning this little girl."

"Go on," Graylin urged.

"That was the end of the dream, but here's the wild thing. After school today, some kids asked me to join their study group. For calculus."

"I've heard wilder."

"It was Ty, Nikki, Morgan, Steph and Mike."

"Okay. And?"

"And we all go to Ty's house. And I *saw* that little girl from my dream. It's Ty's little sister, whom I'd never seen before."

"Matt, it was just a dream. And did you just say 'whom'?"

"Except I'm telling you, it wasn't just a dream! It couldn't have been."

"Look, I don't know how you happened to have seen that little girl in the past, but the brain registers so much and stores it away in the subconscious without us even realizing it. That's all it is. That's all that happened. At some point in time, you saw this girl without realizing it and then your brain kicked her image up for some reason in a dream. Probably after seeing Ty at school. We talked about him that one day. That stuff happens."

"I'm telling you, swearing to you, that I'd never seen her before today," I repeated stubbornly. "Not before the dream. I can't just forget about it. I'm supposed to protect her, somehow."

"From what? Who? Think about it, Matt. I mean, what could you possibly say that wouldn't have people thinking you're a total nut job?"

I scoffed. "People already think I'm a nutjob."

"No, they don't. They think you're a snobby-ass loner, which we both know is bullshit. I'm telling you, you do not have any responsibility toward Ty Larkin's little sister because you had some crazy dream with her in it. How old is she anyway?"

"Like I said, nine or ten, I guess."

"Well, there you go. The killer isn't targeting little girls."

I shook my head in frustration. There was no way I'd get anyone to take me seriously. And I couldn't blame them. I wouldn't have taken me seriously. "All right. Thanks for listening. Just forget I said anything. Okay?"

She hesitated. "Can you forget it?" She sounded worried.

"Honestly? No."

I heard her sigh. "You know what I really think?"

I sat on the arm of a chair feeling miserable. "No," I replied tiredly.

"We all have a some psychic ability. Like you'll think of someone you haven't seen in years and then later that day you see them in person. Right?"

"Yeah. Right."

"Or sometimes I'll be riding down the road without the radio and I'll think of a song. And then I turn on the radio, and there it is. I don't know. Somehow, I knew it was playing right then."

"I know how it all sounds. Everything I was saying about Charlie, but—"

"What?"

"I said I know it sounds crazy, but until I shut the refrigerator door at Ty's house and saw the picture of his little sister, I had never seen her before except in that dream."

"You said *Charlie*?"

"Yeah. Her name is Charlotte, but they call her Charlie. Why?"

Silence.

"Graylin?"

"Yeah, I'm here, but I've … got another call coming in. I'll call you right back."

"Wha—"

"I'll call you right back," she repeated.

She disconnected the call, but I still held my phone for a few seconds, surprised not so much by her hanging up, but by how much energy had just crackled back and forth between us in that last second or two of conversation. As if I'd seriously alarmed her.

Good. I was glad.

"Sorry about that," Graylin said when she called, maybe five minutes later.

"It's okay."

"So, about the dream—"

"Yeah?"

"It was only a dream," she said calmly. "I wouldn't think any more about it."

I couldn't come up with a response for a second, because I hadn't expected to hear that. "Okay," I said slowly. "But, um, if you didn't want to help, why'd you call back?"

"Look, I believe you had a dream, but I think you're making too much of it."

"Really? So, where did you have to go a minute ago?" I asked, suddenly suspicious. "Cause you didn't believe me until I said Charlie's name and—"

"Matt, stop. Okay?"

"No, it's not okay. Look, I don't know why I was given this … obligation, but I was. And you know what? I know the cops are on this and everything, but they haven't found the guy, have they? Maybe I can see things from a whole different perspective or something."

"Well, if you could solve the case, that would be really great, I'm sure. So, what are your thoughts, Sherlock?"

"Sherlock, huh? Should I call you Watson?"

"Absolutely. I'd be delighted to be your Watson."

"Really? It doesn't feel like it."

"Matt, I swear I'm on your side. I just don't want you to be thought of as a—"

"As a freak? Too late."

"Don't be stupid! Nobody thinks of you as a freak. The truth is, you have a great heart, but it may get you into trouble here. I'm just trying to save you from yourself."

"Well, don't."

"Okay. Fine," she snapped.

Talk about painting yourself into a corner. I'd just cut her off when I didn't really want to stop talking. I didn't have anyone else to talk to. "So, that's it?" I said, anyway. Stubborn and stupid, thy name is Matthew Matthews.

"You were sharing your thoughts?"

I'd been granted a reprieve. "I've been thinking about the fact that Madison was found at school," I said grudgingly.

"Yeah. After helping with a cheerleading clinic. And if she hadn't left her ring and gone back for it," she said and then left it hanging. "But what about it?"

I couldn't remember any mention of any cheerleading clinics or rings, and I thought I'd read everything about the case. "My point was going to be that they've got security cameras at school."

"Right."

"Good ones. Surprisingly sophisticated and pretty well concealed. I've been paying attention in the last few days."

"You're right. They're the best in the school system. Maybe the best in the state. Because they were put by a private donor. You know about Laurel Woods?"

"No."

"Of course you don't," she said drolly. "Well, let me just tell you, everyone knows her except for you. She's gorgeous and stuck on herself, but why not? All the guys pant when she walks by. Anyway, when she was a freshman, this guy, another student, began stalking her. So her dad, who's rich; he owns a big advertising firm or something, had a state-of-the-art security system installed throughout the entire school."

"Did they catch the guy?"

"Yeah, they did. And he was expelled."

"My point is," I said, "—that whoever killed Madison had to have been an insider of sorts. Your random guy off the street isn't going to know about those cameras." I waited for a response, but none came. "Still with me?"

"I'm with you."

"The killer had to have known about them, because he either covered the right ones or broke them or something. Because, otherwise, there would be video footage and the guy would have been caught by now."

"What exactly do you mean by insider?"

I shrugged. "Someone who knows the school. A teacher or a student or someone on the staff. Or someone who connected with someone like that." I paused. "I'm thinking a student or maybe a couple of them."

"Why?"

"Well, it can't be a known criminal because their DNA is on file. Right? With what happened to the girls, you know they had to have scratched or pulled hair or something."

"You would think," she agreed.

"Maybe one really strong guy could do it alone, but Madison was an athlete."

"Yeah, she was an awesome gymnast. She could do those backflips across the floor. Made me dizzy just watching."

"Exactly. She was small, but she was strong. And when your life is on the line, adrenalin kicks in making you even stronger. You want to live, so you fight and fight hard."

"Right."

"You know who I was thinking about?"

"Who?"

"Well, after seeing Charlie, I started thinking about Ty. Not him as the bad guy, but remember Dora's gang that was targeting him and his friends?"

"Okay, Matt. Wow. You really cannot accuse—"

"I'm just thinking aloud."

"You can get into serious trouble—"

"Last time I checked, my phone wasn't bugged. I'm just talking to my faithful sidekick, Watson. Speculating. But think about it. Think how creepy they are and how they've targeted Ty and his whole group. I only noticed after Madison died, but she was part of that group. So maybe it started before."

"But it didn't start before."

"There is something seriously off with the whole skunk club. Especially her. And I'll bet she has equally creepy friends outside the school. She could have smuggled one of them in."

"Matt?"

"Yeah?"

"Is it okay if I pick you up in the morning?"

I didn't speak for a second, because I couldn't.

"And we can talk this all out," she continued. "I've got to run for now, but I'll come get you in the morning. Okay?"

"Okay. Sure. Yeah. I live at—"

"I know where you live. Just don't do anything or say anything to anyone else for now. Okay?"

If I was slow to respond, it's because 'I know where you live' was still reverberating around my brain like a crazily careening ping pong ball. "I wasn't going to call a press conference or anything," I finally said.

"I'm serious. You don't know how much trouble you can get into suggesting—"

"Yeah, okay. Got it."

"'Kay."

I racked my brain for how she could possibly know where I lived. I hadn't told her. It's not that I'm ashamed of these shabby apartments but living here doesn't exactly make me glow with pride either. But before I could ask how or even if she really knew the address, she said bye and hung up again.

For a few seconds, I just stared into space. Then, I decided to get out of the apartment and run because I had way too much energy. I layered on a sweatshirt and jacket, added gloves and ear protectors, then stretched, headed outside and took off. If I lived on Ty's street, maybe I would have gone out to shoot hoops, and some of the other guys from the neighborhood might have joined in. Inside, little sisters would play Barbie dolls while moms baked banana nut bread and dads worked on restoring some beloved old car in the garage. That I didn't have that kind of life and would never have it, at least in the role of the son, fueled a long, hard run.

8

Sirena

After my run and a shower, I felt motivated to try another self-hypnosis session. I had managed it before, and I had connected to *something*, because I had never seen Charlie or that swing set before earlier that afternoon. I had to try and go deeper, no matter how bizarre a journey it was.

I got comfortable and relaxed. I looked around my room and noticed my open book bag on the floor. Then I noticed the way the forced air from the floor vent made my curtains billow. I noticed the hole in the toe of my left sock. I kept breathing deeply. In with the good air, out with the bad, deep and slow. I concentrated on that sound. I listened to the wailing of a distant siren. A steady rain had begun falling again and I listened to it.

I concentrated on the irritation of a new blister on the back of my heel. Sore calf muscles. That I felt slightly tired. I also felt relieved that I'd talked to Graylin. The friendship between us felt easy and natural.

I closed my eyes and remembered Ty glancing at me through the rear-view mirror. I remembered the sounds of conversation and laughter as we ate. The pangs of longing and envy I felt walking into the Larkin's kitchen.

Two things.

I pictured Steph when she urged me to the kitchen. I pictured the filled wine rack.

The sound of Charlie's voice. The theme music of Ruaun3.

The shock I'd experienced when I'd seen the photograph of Charlie on the fridge, and then the more profound shock when Tina and Charlie walked in the door.

Three things.

Graylin's expression of concern that first day in the
cafeteria. Steph, when she turned to me in the backseat. Nikki
and Ty kissing.

Graylin's voice, *You really cannot accuse—*
Charlie's voice, *Tyrooone—*
Tina's voice, *You can come over anytime.*
Feelings.
I felt myself walking.
I'm in, I thought again.

And I was. I was in a dark place, so dark I could barely see,
but I *was* walking. As the darkness let up, I heard footsteps
beside me. I looked over, halfway expecting to see Sirena, but it
was Madison and next to her, Ellyn. On my other side was Kaci
Smith. It felt as if we were in league together.

Why? To protect Charlie?

We were in a hallway at a school, but not my school.
Suddenly, I saw bodies of dead and injured students all around
us. They were in the hall, in classrooms, propped against
lockers, splayed out in grotesque, unnatural positions. There
was blood everywhere. It looked like a war zone. Now the only
sound I heard was my own ragged breathing and footsteps.

Hypnosis was a choice, and I could choose to leave. I could
choose to end this. I was in control.

I'd never seen a dead body before, but there was no doubt
about too many that we passed. Their life was over. Their life
force extinguished. Those that were injured looked at me as if
beckoning for help. They were frightened, hurt, bleeding, but
they didn't scream or speak or moan. Or if they did, I couldn't
hear it. I could only hear my own breathing and my hammering
heart. I wanted to stop and help them, but I couldn't. I was
being propelled forward. Was this a hypnotic trance or was it
something else?

I realized we *were* at my school. There were more bodies,
torn and bloody. Only, this time, I recognized some of the faces.
The horror closed in on me like a physical pressure. It was like
being in water too deep. It was silent, absolutely silent, except
for the sound of my blood pulsing in my ears.

Just mine.

I was alone.

I broke into a wild run, wanting to get away from the carnage. I couldn't help anyone. It was too late, and I wanted out. And then I lifted off the ground and I was flying. I was free, outside, heading toward a dark, star-filled sky at an incomprehensible speed. I was scared, but I had no control, NONE, so there was no point in being afraid. Whatever would happen, would happen.

It seemed like I was about to reach the stars when the atmosphere changed. It was lighter and misty as I slowed and began descending so fast, I was sure I'd crash. And die? Abruptly, all movement slowed or maybe stopped. I couldn't be sure because I didn't have my bearings or balance yet.

There were walls around me.

A floor below, and I was standing on it. Standing inside somewhere foreign. My limbs felt wobbly and I was lightheaded. It still felt like I was moving, but I knew I needed to focus.

The light of the place was subdued. The walls alternated between floor-to-ceiling panels of opaque glass and then stone, and all light emanated from the sections of glass and had an amber hue. The ceiling was twenty feet over my head, maybe more, and it didn't seem like a normal ceiling. It seemed like dark, loamy, earth, entrenched with roots. The cool air smelled damp and it felt different. I turned in a slow circle, staring hard, wondering why the place plucked some vague thread of memory. I'd never been here before; I was sure of that, so how could I recognize it?

I took a step, which felt bizarre because my legs were like rubber. I looked down at them accusingly and saw I was naked. I was naked as a freaking jaybird and now everything was beginning to feel real again. I could clearly feel the cool stone floor under my feet. I walked on and reached a wide corridor lined with tall archways that looked as if they might be doorways except for that it was solid where there should have been doors. There were secrets behind them, I was sure. I pressed a hand against each as I passed it.

I stopped abruptly and cocked my head. Danger. I sensed danger. The hairs on the back of my neck stood on end. Some basic survival instinct screamed RUN, so I did. Mindlessly, panicked, only jerking to a halt when I realized thundering footsteps were coming *at* me. *Shit!* I turned and ran the other way and, right away, there was a sound ahead, like air escaping.

One of the stone archways opened and Sirena stood there alarmed and confused. "Hurry," she cried, gesturing me to her.

I bolted through the door, and it closed behind me. I turned back to see the massive stone door turn clear, as if it was a two-ton block of glass. It was just in time to see several *things* run by. All the air in my lungs went AWOL because I recognized them as assassins of Veorwithe. There is no way to describe how freaky and terrifying they are in person.

According to the explanation on the game, they're biologically human or close hybrids but 'acquired' young and raised to hunt, conquer and kill. Or more accurately, slaughter. By maturity, they use their senses differently, more like wild dogs than men. They don't even look human. I was shaken to the core from having come so close.

"They're here," Sirena said.

I turned to her, covering the family jewels with my hands. I couldn't believe I was here with her again *and naked.*

"Where?" A deep male voice boomed around us, making me jump.

"Moving toward the south chamber. Seven of them."

"Got it."

She turned to face me, and she was clearly pissed. "What are you doing here?" she demanded, enunciating clearly.

I opened my mouth to speak, but no words came. I mean, she was there in front of me and furious, and I was naked. It was not a position of strength. "I don't know," I choked out.

"They would have ripped you apart! How the fuck are you here when I didn't bridge you over?"

I was looking at the living, breathing Sirena. I had no idea what state of being I was in, but it wasn't a dream. It felt as real as anything I had ever felt. I couldn't look at her hard enough, because it was her. And, by that, I mean *her*. The girl I love. With beautiful eyes. She hadn't smiled yet, nor did I really see one coming any time soon, but I was sure that when she did, she would have these very particular dimples. It was *her*. How bizarre was it that I'd played Ruaun3 for years and I'd even had a crush on the animated version of her, but I'd never realized she was the girl. Not consciously, anyway.

"Well?" she exploded.

"I don't know," I repeated.

"Are you from Red Mine?" she asked, crossing her arms.

"From wha—No. I don't know what that is."

"S14?"

"*Uhh*, no."

"One of the planets of Bulder Feld?"

"No!"

"Then where? Why aren't you telling me? We don't have time for this! We have to get you back."

I had no idea how to respond to her.

"You shouldn't be here! I thought I'd communicated that. It's too dangerous."

"You thought you'd communicated that?"

"Yes! And I need to know how you managed it without me?"

I shivered as a powerful new realization began to take hold. "What do you mean bridge me over?"

"I said I did *not* bridge you over!"

I took a half step back from her, needing a moment. It was pure shit to be standing there naked. "Sorry, but I'm lost. Like completely fucking lost. And I am so sorry that I'm naked."

"You're disorientated because you overextended yourself," she accused angrily. "Never try getting here again by yourself again! I'll help you back, but you have to promise never to do this again. Ever. For any reason."

"Sirena," I said. I'm not sure why, exactly. Maybe for no other reason than the pleasure of saying her name to her face.

"Matthew," she returned. With sarcasm? Had that been sarcasm? Not that it really mattered. She really knew me somehow.

"I swear to you, I don't understand anything you've said." I was trying hard to remain calm, which is not the easiest thing when you're standing in front of the girl you love for the first time and you are buck naked. Not to mention that a pack of animal-like assassins had been poised to slaughter you only moments earlier. "I don't think I've overextended myself, since it was ... no work to get here. But I only know what I know from the game."

Suddenly, she seemed disgusted. "Do you think I'm impressed by bravado? It was no work to get here?" she mocked. "On your own?"

"I'm not trying for bravado," I said pleadingly. "I don't know how I got here. I don't even know if this is real or just some ... delusion."

She huffed, "Oh, it's real. And those filthy animals would have torn you limb from limb. The corridor would have been drenched with your blood."

This was not going well. "Just ... just tell me one thing. How did we connect?"

She narrowed her eyes at me. They were blue gray.

"I swear to you; all I know is the game," I pleaded.

She was livid. "What game?" she shouted.

I felt a weird tingle of warning or something. I felt weak, like I might possibly pass out. *Please, God, don't let me faint.* I was fucking naked. "Why don't you answer my question and then I'll answer yours."

"We don't have time for this!"

"Please!"

She rolled her eyes. "Fine. I will take two seconds to tell you what you already know. You and I have a psychic bond. I felt your energy for years, so I finally met it. Or maybe you did. It doesn't matter!"

"Those dreams that weren't exactly dreams—"

Her face registered a little confusion. I think she may have been accepting that I really didn't understand what was happening. "Yes, of course. That's how we connect between worlds."

"But what about Charlie? What about the things I was shown?"

She stepped closer, peering into my eyes. "What are you talking about?" she asked urgently.

"The advice you gave me. The murdered girls?"

She looked stunned. "I don't know anything about murdered girls on your planet."

I was at a complete loss. I'd been sure this was real. But it couldn't be.

Sirena sighed slowly as she closed her eyes and bowed her head. For a second, I thought it was exasperation, but then I felt a draining of anxiety from my body and I realized she was calming us. Both of us.

"You give me advice, too," she said soothingly, opening her eyes again. "All the time. It's our energies connecting. When and how we need one another. I don't know anything about any murdered girls on your planet anymore than you probably know anything about disabling the grid in the eighth quadrant. And yet you've given me advice that worked, and strength when I needed it. I don't know how. All I know is that you care as I care for you. Beyond that, I don't have any answers. If I did, I would tell you."

She stepped closer, close enough that I could have kissed her. And, I wanted to.

"Promise that you won't come here again without my help."

What was I going to say to that? I didn't want to lie to her. "I don't want to make you mad, but I can't make that promise. I don't understand any of this, but if there was any way I could do it again and see you again, I'd do it."

She backed up and her eyes flashed. "Do you not understand the danger?"

"No! Probably not. I told you, all I know is what I know from the game."

"What game are you talking about?" she yelled.

"Ruaun3. You're one of the main characters."

She shook her head slowly. "Matt," she appealed. "You're confused because you've overtaxed your ability, whether you realize or not. You are one only half the connection. Even if we've become so fused that you can phase over by yourself, you shouldn't. Maybe there will be a time when it's safe, but that's not now." I was about to reply, but she held up a finger. "I will not argue about this." She stepped up to me and embraced me.

I wasn't sure whether to wrap my arms around her or keep myself covered. I wanted the first but opted for the second, although I leaned in to her.

"Close your eyes," she whispered. "Trust me."

I did. Happily. To my astonishment, I lifted off the ground. My eyes flew open, but I was back in motion and the motion was so crazy fast, my vision blurred. I squeezed my eyes shut again and my stomach lurched. And then all movement abruptly stopped.

I opened my eyes to find myself back in my room, fully dressed as before, still reeling from the momentum. I reached down and clutched my bedspread in my fingers, completely overwhelmed and even more clueless than I had been after the first trance. I also felt really, really alone.

9

The Brat Squad

The next morning, Graylin pulled to a stop in front of my building driving a sweet blue Prius. Three words leapt to mind. Must. Be. Nice. I got inside, we exchanged hellos, and she drove on. "Nice ride," I commented.

"Thanks." She glanced over at me. "About yesterday, are you okay?"

I knew I looked rough because after the experience with Sirena I hadn't been able to sleep. My brain just would not shut off. I'd dozed around four a.m., but I'd never fully given in to it. I shrugged. "Couldn't sleep."

"Matt, you're not crazy."

"No? It does seem to be the question of the hour," I said, looking sideways at her as if I were kidding.

"You're not. You're an extremely bright young man."

I busted out laughing.

"You okay, there, friend?"

"Yeah, sure. Absolutely. And, by the way, I think you're an astute and articulate young woman."

"Damn right, I am. So, now that we've figured that out, we're going to skip school today."

I shook my head. "No can do."

"You can," she assured me. "It'll be okay."

"See, here's the thing. You know how when a child is born, fairies gather and bestow gifts upon them?"

She nodded. "I saw that on Sleeping Beauty."

"Well, in my case, one of them cursed me with the responsibility gene."

She grinned. "I get that. Me, too."

I snorted. "Right." How many classes had she missed?

"Worry not. You're not going to be counted absent."

I suddenly pictured her breaking into the office in the middle of the night and doctoring the attendance records. Or maybe she was a genius hacker who could do it from home. That would explain her getting away with missing so many days, way more than the Gestapo allows. "How are you going to pull that off?"

"It's already done."

"Bullshit."

"Not bullshit." She glanced in the rearview mirror and then pulled over onto the side of the road. She put the car in park and then turned to face me with a serious expression. "I have something to tell you."

"Are you a hacker?"

She drew back. "What?"

"Have you found a way to mess with attendance records?"

"I do not commit illegal actions. Other than speeding occasionally, but only if there's a good reason or a really great song on."

"And I suppose I'm going to get your scout's honor on this?"

"Matt?"

"What?"

"I'm enrolled at North as part of an undercover operation."

"Look, I hate being a goody-two-shoes, if that's what it seems like, but—"

"I'm serious. I am enrolled at North High School as part of an undercover operation."

I experienced a painful chill as I suddenly wondered if *she* was a delusion. That movie *A Beautiful Mind* was based on a true story. John Nash was brilliant, a Nobel prize winner in economics, and his delusions had seemed so real to him, he hadn't known they were only figments of his imagination for years. Oh, wow. All the wild stuff that had been happening to me lately. Was it possible I'd I only imagined them? *No!* I was not crazy. I wasn't interesting enough to be crazy. Besides, he was a genius. I am no genius.

"I'm not eighteen, I just look it," Graylin continued. "Makes me the perfect candidate."

"For what?"

"What do you mean for what? For posing as a high school student, numb nuts."

I kept looking at her, waiting for the punch line.

"I'm a junior SBI agent," she stated.

"SBI," I repeated.

She nodded. "The State Bureau of Inves—"

"I know what it stands for. I'm just—" I shook my head. "Just ... keep talking."

"I graduated from State last year with a degree in criminal justice and got the car as a graduation gift. My family doesn't have a lot of money, but they saved, and it was from everyone. My parents, my grandparents, our neighbors, my aunts and uncles, etcetera, etcetera. The thank you cards took me three days to write."

For some reason, this quasi-defensive personal tidbit made me like her even more.

"Anyway, I was lucky enough to be accepted into the bureau right after graduation."

I could suddenly picture it. For real. "That must have been a thrill."

"Oh, yeah. You have no idea how many times I stood in front of a full-length mirror flashing my badge when I first got it. I almost threw my shoulder out. Of course, the work itself was less thrilling. I was assigned to the computer crimes unit, which is not exactly the stuff action-thrillers are made of. But, after the Smith murder, they pulled seven of us newbies from various divisions to go into the high schools of this county and learn what we could. The rest of the Bureau calls the brat squad. Nice, huh?"

It actually was the stuff TV series were made of, and yet I believed her. I also believed in my own mind and experiences, no matter how bizarre they had been of late.

"I know how it must sound."

"I believe you," I stated. "What I don't get is, what do they think you can do? They're not using you as bait, are they?"

"I can't tell you much, but I can tell you there are reasons for everything."

"Is the reason that if you have a pool of victims, it makes sense to jump into the pool?"

"I'm going to take you to headquarters now."

I felt a jolt of alarm. "Why?"

"Let's just say that you knew something that buys you a day pass into my world." She faced front, put the car into gear, checked her mirrors, and pulled back out.

"What was it about learning Charlie's name that—"

She stuck her hand in the air. "Hold up, buttercup. It'll be a whole lot easier to have this conversation at the office."

"I'm really not going to be counted absent?"

"Cross my heart and hope to die."

I thought about it. "You know, given recent events, that's a really, creepy phrase."

She wrinkled her nose. "You've got a point."

Wow. She was an agent. An *agent*. "Kind of an unusual career path for you, isn't it?"

She pulled her shades down on her nose and gave me a pointed look. "The director of the SBI is a woman, so is one of the one of the assistant directors."

"I didn't mean the female thing. It's more that you're petite and—"

"*And* I can tackle and cuff a three-hundred-pound man in under a minute if I see him coming."

"Duly noted."

She frowned quizzically as she tapped her sunglasses back in place. "Why does that phrase make me crave Doritos?"

When we pulled into the entrance of a nondescript, brown brick building, it occurred to me that the place was so unremarkable, I'd never noticed it. Graylin parked and we walked toward a back entrance. She swiped a card to gain access, the door buzzed, and we went inside. The hall was quiet and empty. The metal doors that lined the hall were all shut and few of them were labeled with names. The few that were identified were nothing I'd ever heard of.

"Fair warning, my boss can be kind of a jerk," Graylin confided in a hushed tone.

The knot in my stomach tightened. "Now you mention this," I muttered.

She smirked. "It'll be okay. I won't let him hurt you or anything."

"So I guess you can do all that martial arts stuff?"

"Oh, yeah. And leap off tall buildings." She grinned and opened the fourth door on the left. I followed her into a mid-sized room filled with a long table, chairs and blank bulletin boards. I smelled fresh coffee and spotted an open box of donuts. The three people in the room, a girl and two guys, all looked to be about my age. They watched me with interest.

"This is Matt," Graylin announced. "He's my compatriot, so be nice to him. Want a donut?" she asked me. "Help yourself. I'll go get everybody."

One guy immediately followed Graylin into another room, talking in a clandestine tone as they went. The other two had been working on their laptops. "I'm Caleb," a curly-haired guy with glasses said. "Welcome to the cocoon."

"Thanks."

"Laura," the girl said with a friendly smile.

"Hello," I said. I stood for a moment, feeling awkward as hell, and then I went for a donut. I've never been known to pass up a donut and I probably never will. I chose a jelly filled with a coating of white icing and bit into it. I enjoyed moments of pure, mindless sugar-bliss until I saw the raspberry filling had dripped onto my white sweatshirt. I mouthed an expletive and reached for a napkin.

"You might want to get some cold water on that," Laura suggested.

"Don't feel bad, man," Caleb said. "Personally, I never eat or drink anything I don't end up wearing."

"Water cooler," Laura said, pointing to it.

I inhaled the rest of the donut as I walked to the water cooler. I got a little water on the napkin, rubbed the stain deeper into my shirt, then gave up and wiped my hands.

Great.

"You know, you could drip a lot of jelly on it," Caleb offered. "Make it look like a design."

Laura groaned. "Only you, Caleb."

"I tried it once with mustard," Caleb admitted. "Come to think of it, it didn't turn out so well. People would look at the shirt and go, is that *mustard*?" He looked over at me and then at Laura, as if he was insulted. "Uh, *no*."

A back door opened and Graylin came back into the room with three other people, two guys who looked a little older than me and a man in his early thirties.

"This is Randy Johnson," Graylin said to me, referring to the older guy. "Boss man."

I almost stuck out my hand, but Randy crossed his arms. He didn't appear to be the particularly friendly sort.

"And this is Frank," Graylin said, pointing to one of the guys, "and Shawn," she said, gesturing to a good-looking black guy with long braids.

Shawn offered his hand. "I hear you're a young agent in the making."

"I don't know about that," I replied as I shook his hand. I suspected that Shawn was one of *those* guys, a natural born star. Easygoing, athletic and intelligent, but not in-your-face with it. And Graylin had been right; they all looked young.

"And this is my friend, Matt," Graylin finished.

Randy perched on the edge of the table. "Are you psychic, Matt?" he asked with an edge to his voice.

My initial instinct was that Randy was the opposite of Shawn. Yeah, he was the boss at the moment, but he had to work at it, the job, the image and all the other stuff. He wanted to be cool, but there was just something lacking. "No, sir."

"So, how did you know about Charlie?"

I glanced at Graylin, who looked apologetic, and then back to Randy Johnson, and explained my dream. I wasn't telling anyone I'd seen a vision of Charlie in a trance.

"Let's just say, for a second, that I buy that," Randy said. "What made you suspect Dora?"

I opened my mouth to explain that it wasn't Dora I suspected so much as the goons she hung with, but something about Randy Johnson's intensity made me shut up. "Her behavior. The spite. That kind of hate is … it's not natural."

"*Uh-huh.* Well, here's what you need to know. We're taking what you said seriously. As it turns out, we already had cause to do that."

"Because you knew Charlie's name, somehow," I guessed.

Randy gave Graylin an accusing look. "What did you say?"

"I didn't say anything, although you just confirmed it," Graylin countered.

"He's got the instinct," Shawn said as if he was enjoying himself.

"Well, listen up, Mister *Instinct*," Randy said to me, no less agitated than before. "You are not to say anything to anyone about anything."

"Uh, Randy?" Caleb said. "What if he gets called on in class?"

It was then I noticed all the junior agents had their arms crossed exactly like Randy. I nearly smiled at the display of solidarity.

Randy glared at Caleb and then looked back at me. "Got it?"

"I do," I replied. "I wasn't going to say anything. But may I ask how you knew about Charlie?"

"Yes, you may ask. And, no, we're not telling you."

"Well, when you say you're taking it seriously, what does that mean? That you're protecting her? You have her under surveillance?"

"That's right. And more than that, I will not say." He looked pointedly at Graylin. "Nor will anyone else if they value their job."

"So, basically," Graylin said to Randy, "you had me bring him in to tell him we're on it and to keep his mouth shut." She looked pissed.

"That's right."

"Actually, that's kinda' wrong," Frank said to Randy. "At least, in my humble opinion."

"Well, thanks," Randy gushed. "You telling me means I won't spend a sleepless night wondering about it."

"Hey, Matt," Caleb spoke up. "Seriously, what made you think about Dora and the dorks? I mean, I know they're jerks, but high school is full of them." He glanced at the others. "As if we didn't learn that well enough the first time around, here we are again."

"It was more than that," I said. "I saw them go out of their way to torment friends of Madison's. Like it was a personal vendetta. Which made me wonder if they'd hated Madison as much as they apparently hate Ty and rest of his group."

"This is an official investigation," Randy said as he got to his feet. "Interfere in any way—"

"I won't," I assured him.

He stalked from the room.

"Let's go," Graylin said to me.

"Like water off a duck's back," Shawn said under his breath, directing it to Graylin.

She shook her head as she walked off and I followed.

"Hey, Matt," Caleb called. "Sure you don't want to grab another donut? I was serious about that design thing. You might have more luck than I did."

I grinned, despite Randy's slap down. "I'm good. Thanks."

"See ya, Matt," Frank said.

"I'm sorry about that," Graylin said on our way back to school. "I'm downgrading Randy's status from jerk to complete fucking asshole."

"I'm sure he thinks he's just doing his job."

"Yeah, and the rest of us are …what? Kicked back, eating bonbons?"

She was really pissed. Which made me feel good. "All those empty bulletin boards," I started.

"They're not empty. They were turned around so you wouldn't see what's on them."

"What does 'water off a duck's back' mean?"

"That was just a reminder not to take Randy too seriously. When he gets all full of himself and shooting off at the mouth, his words become as important to us as water off a duck's back. They roll right off."

"Gotcha."

We didn't speak any more until we pulled in the school parking lot and she turned off the ignition. "You didn't even miss a full block. I'm sorry. That whole thing was pretty unnecessary."

"It's okay. AP History is pretty unnecessary."

She grinned.

"Are you staying?"

Her top lip curled. "I guess."

"So, we'll do lunch."

"I'll pencil you in."

I shifted to face her. "Do the teachers know who you are?"

"I don't think so. Administration does, of course."

"Which is how you can miss so many days, I guess."

"Yeah, well, having graduated from high school and college with honors, thank you very much, grades don't matter a whole hellova' lot at this point. Nor do missed days."

"Must be nice."

She put a hand on my arm. "Hey, you ever desperately need a day off, you let me know. Okay? We owe you."

"How do you owe me? Did I tell you anything you didn't already know?"

She looked regretful. "I can't talk about it."

"It's okay. I'm just glad someone's watching out for Charlie."

She nodded. "We are."

75

"Is it a total nightmare to be back in high school?"

"It's not really like that," she replied, shaking her head. "I'm not *back*. I'm pretending to be someone who's here. It's different."

"Is it?"

"Completely," she exclaimed. "This doesn't feel like the high school experience I had at all," she clarified. "It feels … meaner. More closed off, I guess."

"You mean kids talking shit about other kids? Like Suzy Slut?"

"Yeah. Like that. And like spending every other minute staring at your cell phone. Drawing validation from social media. I fear that it's destroying the minds of our youth."

I had to laugh. "What is the story on Suzy Slut, anyway?"

She raised a brow. "Getting interested in gossip, are we?"

"No, but lately I've begun to feel like I really have lived on another planet for the last year. Everybody's talking about everybody, and I've got no clue."

"That's what I like about you. But I guess your innocence had to go sometime. So, this girl, Suzanne Farlow, got involved with this total asshole named Hunter Hultberg."

"Is that his real name?"

"Yep. And who knows why, but she sexted him. You know, sent a picture of her very most private self," she finished with a southern accent.

"And it got out to the public?"

"He sent it out," she exclaimed disgustedly. "See, that's what kills me. He does that, and she becomes the social outcast of the universe. Suzy Slut. I hear that and I just want to slam somebody's head into a locker."

I nodded, because it's how I feel about people making fun of Toby. "Did she even go by Suzy?"

"I don't know. I don't think so. Just catchier that way."

Catchy. Never before had the word seemed so grimy. "Man, once I get out of here, you couldn't pay me enough to come back. How do you stand it?"

She shrugged. "It's my job. I'm getting paid. *And* there's a good reason for being here. *And* I've met a few people worth knowing." She stuck her hand up and I slapped it. "Now let's get in there and larn something," she finished, using the voice of a southern drill sergeant.

Such a goofball.

That afternoon, Steph cornered me at my locker and asked if Graylin was 'the one.' Steph looked really pretty in a pale pink sweater and a short jean shirt. She also looked vulnerable. "No. Not the one I mentioned to you," I replied. "We're just friends."

"Oh," was all she commented, but it said a lot.

I felt badly, but there were a lot of things pressing in on me. The events of the last few days had been overwhelming. It felt like I was testing the ground before every step I took, and I still wasn't sure the floor was going to hold.

10

The Convening

I tried self-hypnosis a bunch of times over the next week, but it didn't work. A few times, I felt a trance begin, and then, wham, I'd be fully conscious again. Sitting on my bed back at square one. On a Thursday night, I went to sleep pretty easily, but woke a few hours later. I felt a presence in the room, which was weird. I turned over and found Sirena was sitting on the side of my bed watching me. She had on my t-shirt, one from a stack of clean ones I hadn't put up yet. It didn't look like she was wearing anything but my t-shirt.

"Sorry to wake you," she said quietly.

I sat up. "No, it's fine," I stammered, trying to come fully awake. "I've wanted to see you. I've been trying to connect."

"I know. I've had to block you. It isn't safe."

She looked troubled. "What's wrong?"

"You mentioned a game."

I nodded. "Yeah."

"I thought you were confused because you'd pushed beyond your limits," she said questioningly.

I shook my head. "No. There's a game. I can show you."

"I can't stay," she said urgently. "Will you cross back with me?"

Excitement coursed through me. "Yeah! Of course, but you should see this." I got up and went to my computer and tapped it back to life. I reached for the game case and handed it her.

She stared at it uncomprehendingly. "I don't understand."

I cursored over to the Ruaun3 icon, pressed it, and the theme music drew her attention. Her eyes widened as her own likeness appeared on screen. I pressed Skip Intro as a matter of routine.

"Choose your level," the virtual Sirena said.

"We should go," the real Sirena said. She handed the game box back while continuing to stare at the screen. "We need to ask you some questions."

As I took the case and set it aside, she held out her hands. I took hold of them and immediately felt that sense of flight and velocity. When it stopped, we were in a house or an apartment I'd never seen. I stayed perfectly still, because I wasn't sure how stable I was. Damn it! I was naked again. "Feeling a little movement still," I said.

"It will pass."

She backed up a step and my hands flew to cover myself. "And I am naked again," I said under my breath.

"We'll always be naked on arrival. It's alright, I have something for you to wear," she said, walking away. She returned with what looked like gray active wear, keeping her gaze averted. She turned away as I fumbled to put them on. "There are shoes, too," she said, gesturing to a pair.

"Thanks."

"This is my lodge."

After my pants were on, I felt better. Next came a shirt and then there was a long, tunic-like jacket. The heavy cloth, boot-like shoes felt tight at first and then they didn't. "Ready," I said.

She turned back to face me. There were a few moments of slightly embarrassed awareness of one another and then I looked around the room. A fire burned in a stone hearth, two modern art looking chairs were positioned in front of it. The place was cozy and feminine, but also minimalist. We were in a living room and the bedroom was on a slightly higher level. "This is nice."

"Are you feeling more stable yet?"

I nodded slowly. "I think so. I think I'm getting the hang of … whatever you call it."

"Evup," she said

"Evup," I repeated.

"It's short for evanessport," she replied. "Bringing you here."

"Ah."

"Let's sit for a minute."

As we moved to the chairs and sat, she toyed with an amulet she wore around her neck, looking nervous and surprisingly innocent. The rendition of her in the game is so flashy and exaggerated, it's almost insulting. She doesn't sport double D's. "In some ways, I feel like I know you," I commented, "but, it's also kind of like we're strangers."

"That's because we're both fully conscious. Usually, one of us is only semi-conscious and, in that state, you feel the essence of a person but not the full force of them."

I nodded as if we'd just exchanged comments about the weather.

"I'll explain what's happening here," she said, "—and then take you to meet the others. Although, I'm not sure where to begin. I don't know what you know."

"Why don't you assume I know the basics and go from there," I suggested.

"But do you?"

"I know the game."

"The game," she repeated. "Matt, we fear this game may be our problem, which is why we need to understand it."

"What do you mean?"

"Too many of us are suddenly being tagged or disappearing. We can't help wondering if there's a traitor amongst us. Or maybe they were with us and then they left and created this game, which really isn't a game at all, but some sort of code revealing who and where we are." She paused and worried her bottom lip. "It's been pointed out how little I know about you," she admitted.

I felt a pang of foreboding.

"I just need you to tell me before I take you over."

She wanted to protect me. "Okay."

"Starting with where you live."

"North Carolina."

She looked puzzled. "Where?"

"I live in a town outside kind of a small city in North Carolina." She still looked baffled. As if I was talking gibberish. "North Carolina," I said, half kidding. "Which is a state in the southeast. Of the United States." She still looked lost. "Which is a country in North America," I added almost teasingly. I couldn't get a handle on her confusion. "On the planet Earth."

Her jaw dropped. Her shock was palpable.

I almost laughed but, on second thought, her reaction wasn't funny.

"Earth!"

My heart was hammering. "Yes."

"What year?" she asked breathlessly.

What year? What the fuck? "2008."

She let out a gush of breath. Her eyes filled with tears, and she stood straight up. She began to pace nervously. "It never occurred to me. How is it even possible?" She stopped abruptly and then turned to face me. "We must be positioned at a TCS."

I felt tingly in a new and highly unpleasant way. "A what?"

"A time continuation stutter. A break in the flow of time."

"A time warp? Is that what you're saying? They're real?"

"They're extreme anomalies. Only two, maybe three, have been discovered in our entire solar system."

I took a couple of breaths before I asked, "Is it really twenty-eight-thirteen here?"

She frowned. "2818."

I took a minute to process this. The best I can explain it is that, deep down, even after all she'd said and everything I'd experienced, I'd still thought of Ruaun3 as some sort of fantasy realm until that minute. But it wasn't. This was a real place, and she was real and very much alive. I was about to meet real people who had a real life or death dilemma. This was reality made manifest by some sort of metaphysical, psychic link between the two of us. It was mind blowing and yet I felt the pieces of the puzzle slipping into place. As bizarre as it was, it made sense to me.

"I thought you were on another planet," she said apologetically.

"I thought you were a gorgeous character in a game. So that explanation that comes up when I turn the game on, that earth became uninhabitable around 2500 AD. Is that true?"

She hesitated a moment before nodding. She sat back down. "I'm sorry."

"And, after that, everyone moved out to man-made planets?"

"Everyone who survived Eternal Day."

I couldn't speak for a moment and then I cleared my throat and gave it a shot because I needed to know how factual the explanation on the game actually was. "Hundreds of planets were created, but some flourished more than others. Ruaun3 is one of the more desirable."

She nodded.

"Around 2810, the Foundation took over and started QFRs, so a rebellion began. They call you hoods."

"The Resistance, Hoods. They have several names for us. Do you know anything about how we're organized?"

"What do you mean?"

"Are Tiers mentioned anywhere in the game?"

I shook my head. "I've never heard anything about tiers."

"Good. The ... people in the game, the characters, besides me, who are the others?"

"On our side—" I faltered because I realized how lame that sounded, but Sirena hadn't reacted. "Um, there's Dairy and Ji, Ocean, Aiden, Smoke—"

"These are real people! And we're not all groundlings."

"Groundlings?"

"We're not all underground. Some of us live in the open. Do you understand the danger? Of exposure? Exposure means death. A bad death." She rose and took a few steps away and then back. "Imagine discovering that someone had made a *game* of your life and, in this game, the most secret, dangerous mission that you've built your entire life around was revealed."

I nodded slowly. "You're wondering who created the game because they knew and revealed so much. But it has to be someone in my world, so—"

"No, it has to be someone from our world. Or someone who can cross over. But who can do that? Or it's possible they did cross over—"

"If it's only in my world and in my time, how can it be a threat to anyone here and now?"

She shook her head. "I ... don't know. I didn't know you were from another time."

"Do the others think that I'm the bad guy here?"

She hesitated.

"I'm not!"

"I know that," she stated calmly. "They just need to understand where you've come from and what you know. Not that explaining is going to be easy."

I shrugged and shook my head. "We'll just tell them."

"Matt, it's one thing to bridge from planet to planet. Many of us can do that. But to get to another planet through a time warp? Not only to pass through, but to connect the way we have?" She shook her head. "If someone else had suggested it, I would have said it was impossible. I would have *sworn* it was impossible. Now, I find out we've being doing it. I still can't fully believe it. And I certainly don't understand it."

There was a knock on her door and we both turned as it opened. Not only did I recognize Teddy at once, I felt a chill up my spine to see him in person, especially as he locked me in an intense gaze as he stepped inside.

"Yes, he's here," Sirena said to him. "And there is a game. I saw it." She turned to me, apologetically. "I'm sorry, this is—"

"Teddy," I said. "I know. I've seen his face a lot."

"That's odd, when I've never seen yours," Teddy returned.

Sirena sighed. "I just learned that Matt is from Earth."

He frowned suspiciously. "What are you talking about?"

"He lives on Earth. In the year 2008."

He looked at me and then back at her. "That's impossible."

"It can't be impossible because it's true."

"Have you considered that he's a deceiver?"

Her chin rose slightly. "He is not."

Silence filled the room. *Shit,* I thought.

"They're waiting," he said in a flat voice. "But Xia should read him."

"Fine," Sirena replied. "If you don't believe me."

"It's not that," he snapped.

"Let's go," Sirena said.

I stood, no easy feat, and Sirena gave me an encouraging nod before leading the way out. Cool air hit the instant I stepped outside, but the clothes I was wearing instantly adjusted. Above us, stars and planets were so much bigger, more colorful and plentiful than I'd ever imagined, I stopped and gawked. "Whoa."

"This way," Sirena said, hurrying me on.

I followed her toward a circular ring of dense, spiky-looking trees. Glancing around, the other lodges I saw seemed small and non-descript, but they glowed from light within. Inside the grove of trees was darker. In the center was a mound that was too perfectly symmetrical to be natural. Teddy went to it, held out his hand, and a door opened revealing steps leading down and glowing amber light from within. Sirena went first, I followed, and Teddy came last. At the base of the stairs was a corridor. We hadn't gone far when I recognized the walls made of stone and then opaque glass. I'd been there.

My vision suddenly wavered and I felt so dizzy, I tried to stop and stand still for a second, but there was still movement all around me, as if I was on some crazy moving sidewalk.

"Seery, stop," Teddy said.

All movement stopped and I swallowed hard. We were in a totally different place than before. I felt Teddy's hand on my shoulder.

"Are you all right?" he asked.

"You said everyone was waiting," Sirena said.

"Obviously, he's not used to that," Teddy chastised.

"Oh, all the sudden, you're protecting him? What if he *is* used to it? What if he is a deceiver?"

"I didn't say I thought he was. But why not establish he's telling the truth from the beginning?"

Sirena walked on without response and I suddenly knew she'd somehow moved us forward and she'd done it for a reason that had nothing to do with concern for other people's time. She wanted Teddy on our side. "What do you use for money here?" I asked. My mind was racing through possibilities for the creation of a game that exposed people. "For currency?"

Sirena fell back to walk beside me, curious about the question. "Besides black market currency, all we have is voucher points good for interplanetary vouchers. Why do you ask?"

"I was wondering if money was could motivation for creating the game."

Sirena shook her head. "There's far more bartering than voucher exchange since The Foundation took over. They control everything. They ruined our economy to control us."

"How much money could a game generate?" Teddy asked skeptically. "Although I don't understand what you mean by game."

I halted to answer him. "Video," I said. "It's electronic and can be played on a computer or a TV. And you, meaning the player, controls what's happening on the screen by a controller, like the cursor on the computer or a joystick." They were both watching me blankly. "The game has made a vast amount of money," I replied. "Ruaun3 is a best seller and has been for years."

Teddy shook his head. "On your planet. Not here. Transporting anything of substance between planets and through a time warp is either impossible or ... next to it. There can't possibly be a handful of people in all the seventeen galaxies known that could do that."

Seventeen galaxies?

Sirena looked at me and nodded as if I'd asked it aloud. "Seventeen with civilizations that we know of. There are millions more that we don't know much about." She looked at teddy and back at me. "But he's right. Transporting anything through a time warp might as well be impossible if it's not."

I felt myself sway as everything around me grew wavy. Sirena grabbed my arm. "Are you all right?"

I felt weak.

"Take my hands," Sirena commanded.

I held mine out, but I couldn't see straight. I felt her hands grasp and tighten around mine and my vision cleared. She'd given me strength somehow.

"Shit," Teddy said under his breath.

Sirena gave me a questioning look and I nodded back.

"Let's go," she said.

When we heard voices ahead, my heart began hammering. We entered a large room where people had gathered, at least twenty and maybe more, all of whom stared at me with unabashed curiosity. Only a second before, there had been conversation going on, now there was weighty silence. My mouth went dry as the three of us stopped.

"This is Matt," Sirena announced. "He is my friend and psylink."

"Hello, Matt," a woman said. It was Dairy. "Sirena's friend and psylink."

It was beyond bizarre to see Dairy in person. To see all of them. I nodded, because my throat was too painfully tight to utter a sound.

"Point out anyone you recognize from the game," Sirena suggested to me.

"Is there really a game?" a guy asked. I didn't recognize him.

"Yes," Sirena and I said at the same instant. "I saw it," she added. "I don't know how to describe it, but I saw it."

"Give us an idea," someone said.

"A surveillance screen with moving, animated images of us," she replied. She turned to me, wanting me to name people.

I looked at the solidly built black man standing with his arms crossed. "Aidan," I said,

"You know me on sight," Aidan remarked with displeasure. His deep, resonant voice had been exceptionally well captured on the game.

"Who else?" Sirena asked.

"That's Gabe and Westin," I said, nodding in the direction of the twins.

"Ah, but which of us is which?" one asked sardonically.

"Shut up, Westin," Dairy said.

"You're Dairy," I said, naming her.

"Son of a bitch," Dairy murmured with a disgusted frown.

"Oh, and, by the way," I said, turning back to the twins. "That one's Westin," I said, gesturing to the one Dairy had outed.

"Funny," Westin approved with a smirk. "I like that. He may be a plant and a spy, but at least he's an amusing one."

"He's not a plant or a spy," Sirena retorted.

"I don't think so either," Teddy offered.

The relief I felt to have his support was profound. "You're Ocean," I continued, gesturing to a light skinned black guy who looked to be a few years older than me. "And you're Smoke," I said, nodding politely to the most beautiful woman I have ever laid eyes on. The game had made her gorgeous and it hadn't done her justice.

"Names and faces," Dairy exclaimed to Aiden. "No wonder we're being targeted."

"Who made this fucking game?" Aidan roared furiously.

"We have to get our hands on it," Dairy said.

"It's not here," Sirena spoke up.

Everyone looked at her.

"It's played in Matt's world …on technology we don't use."

"What technology does another planet have that we don't?" Aiden asked with an insulted expression.

"It's more an issue of … time," Teddy spoke up.

"Time," Dairy repeated.

Teddy nodded. "Matt is from … Earth."

I saw confusion and disbelief all around.

"A lot of us are from Earth," Aiden said slowly. "Or our ancestors were."

"You don't understand," Sirena said. "He lives there. Currently."

Aiden looked ready to explode. "No one has lived on Earth for more than three hundred years!"

"He lives there, currently," Teddy reiterated calmly. "Which, for him, is the year 2008."

No one moved or spoke. Smoke took a step forward. "Are you saying—"

"I'm saying Matt lives on Earth in 2008," Teddy stated.

Everyone's gaze was on me.

"Assuming we believe that—" Aiden said.

"Why would he lie?" Dairy posed without looking away from me with those piercing violet eyes. "How about we *assume* and move the fuck on."

"Sirena would know if it wasn't true," Smoke said. "And she would say."

"That's right," Sirena spoke up. "I would."

Aidan shook his head. "You tell me something that's impossible and then expect me to swallow it ... because?"

"It's not exactly impossible," Ocean mused thoughtfully. "Although I don't fully get it yet." He looked at Sirena. "You two have linked for a while now, yes?"

Sirena nodded.

"Huh," Ocean replied under his breath. "I think it means someone discovered a path, a wormhole, locked into it and—"

"Who's done that?" a guy I didn't know asked. "Locked onto a wormhole? We'd know about it. Everyone would know. It would have made history."

Ocean shrugged. "I don't see any other way it's possible."

Smoke came toward me. "Tell us about this game." The last word was spoken with a little curl to her lip as if the word disgusted her. "What's the object?"

"That depends on which side you take," I replied. "You can choose to be Hood, that's you guys, or Foundation. You either make up a character or choose to play as ... one of you."

"Or one of the Foundation," she said. "Correct?"

"No, if you choose to be FO, you have to make an avatar."

88

"Then their identities aren't revealed in the game?" Smoke asked. "You know ours, but not theirs?"

"Well, there's Cutter, of course. There's a guy named Dyken, sometimes he's called Captain Dyken. There's Letters, a fat man with a British accent. But you can't play as any of them."

"Letters?" another guy spoke up. "Who the hell is Letters?"

"Go on," Aidan said, his dark-eyed gaze never wavering from mine.

"Except for them, and generic looking FO's, there's only the assassins of Mount Veorwithe."

"What's the object of the game if you're Foundation?" Ji asked. I hadn't noticed him before, but I recognized him from the game, of course. He has cook, tilted eyes and olive skin.

"To find and kill rebels."

"And if you're one of us?" Teddy asked.

"You have to stop QFRs, take out officials, win skirmishes. Battle and beat the assassins of Mount Veorwithe. Escape from raids. Of course, the ultimate goal is to get into the maze and somehow take out the powers that be, but I've never made it that far. I can't tell you who they are."

Smoke looked over at Dairy. "It sounds as if the creator of the game knows our side, but not theirs."

"You've been there?" Aiden asked Sirena. "To Earth?"

"Yes."

"In 2008?" Smoke said. "You passed through a warp and made it back?"

"I didn't realize it, but yes. I thought ... I thought Matt was simply on another planet."

"Do you know who created the game?" Ji asked me.

Of course I knew, but my mind was fuzzy all of the sudden. A sick fatigue was overtaking me. "Um, a company called Marsh-Singledon," I managed sluggishly. "I can try and find out more."

"Anything you can do," Sirena said to me. Weakly.

Her voice was so strange. I looked over and saw she looked pale and shaky. I needed to sit down.

"Sirena?" Dairy called.

Sirena shook her head. *I can't hold you,* she thought. She reached out for me and I tried to reach for her, but I was caught up in a mad rush of light and movement. I didn't know up from down until I found myself in my own bed.

It was mid-morning.

I sat up, still reeling, and grabbed a pillow. I hugged it to me and rocked back and forth, trying to process everything. It was 9:30, which meant I was late for school. I stood and then had to sit again, I was so weak. I carefully got up and went downstairs for something to eat, but there was no milk, no eggs, no generic cereal or generic pop-tarts. Only a stale heel was left in the loaf of bread. I was usually better about keeping up with groceries. I toasted the bread and added peanut butter and jelly and devoured it before carrying a glass of water back upstairs with me.

I rebooted the computer and went to work to learn all I could about the creators of the game. I found a lot of information on the game itself, but there was surprisingly little about the game designer. Finally, I found it. He was a man named Cres Singledon, and he was one of only two principals of the multi-million-dollar company. He was purported to be under thirty, brilliant and reclusive, which explained the lack of interviews. The full bio of the other principal, Ed Marsh, was available, but it didn't interest me much. I'd read enough to know he was the money guy and Singledon the creative end.

I only found one photograph of Singledon taken by a magazine at a launch party and it wasn't an up-close shot. From what I could tell, he was a good-looking guy with brown hair and a shy but mischievous looking smile that reminded me of someone, but I couldn't place who. Probably some actor I'd seen. I have a black and white printer, but it's not great quality, nor was the photograph, but I printed it and also saved the image under My Favorites.

The last thing I did was to email Marsh-Singledon's customer service department through their 'contact us' page and request an interview with Singledon. I claimed I was a big fan, which is true, and that I wanted to do my high school senior project on PC game development, which could conceivably be true.

It was 10:35. I got up to get ready for school, since I could still make my last two classes. I was feeling less weak and off-balance since I was firmly rooted here and now.

Even if I wished otherwise.

11

Valentine's Day. Yay.

Insane or not insane, that is the question. Each sojourn to Ruaun3 feels as real as this existence. And right afterwards, it still feels that way, but then a day goes by and then another and then another and I start second guessing myself. Still, every day, I wonder what's happening there. I wonder what I'd be doing if I was there. I wonder what Sirena is doing.

Instead, I'm jammed in a crowded hallway on Valentine's day in a sea of red sweaters and pink shirts and fruity-smelling heart shaped suckers that student council is selling. I know it's supposed to be this ooey-gooey sweet, romantic day, but I've always thought it was supremely idiotic. I'd bet good money they don't celebrate Valentine's Day on Ruaun3. If they did and if I was there, I might feel differently about it, but I wouldn't give Sirena a heart shaped card and red-cellophane box of chocolates.

Or maybe I would.

Actually, I probably would. I would love to do that.

One of the main things I loathe about high school is the congested halls between classes. It's always the same. The bell rings, the halls fill up, everyone having to get here or there, and yet you always have jerks who clump in the middle, forcing everyone to go around them. It's all about getting attention. I'm just trying to get to chemistry.

The sharp contrast of black and white against all the precious pink got my attention. Dora and co were closing in on Nikki as she stood getting something from her locker. I changed direction, swam against the tide of traffic and stepped between them. "Hey," I said to Nikki.

She smiled to see me, but then the freak show behind me caught her eye.

"Just get your stuff," I said lightly. "Don't look at them. Don't give the satisfaction."

Woodenly, she turned back to her locker and got her stuff.

"Where are you going?" I asked.

"French."

My presence didn't derail the skunk club. "Nikki want a licky?" Dora said behind us.

I didn't budge. "They want to get a rise out of you," I told Nikki. "That's all. They're leeches who want to clamp onto to somebody who actually has a life."

I felt a hard jab in the center of my back. Fingertips. Dora's. I turned and she was practically right up against me. She had a sucker in her hand which she'd been licking on. "You talking shit about me?" she asked, just above a whisper.

I got the feeling this was her pose of seduction, although what species would be attracted to her, I didn't have a clue. "Who you?" I asked just as softly, giving her the once over. "Who would talk shit about you? It would be like talking shit about … a stink bug. I mean, what's the point?"

Her cronies did this half-laughing, half-warning huffing and puffing thing. I didn't even glance at them.

Dora twisted the heart-shaped sucker back and forth in front of my face. "How do you think this would feel shoved up your ass?" she asked quietly, her eyes gleaming.

"About like you do," I said, taking a step backwards with a look of disgust. "Too close for comfort."

When Nikki and I started off, Ty and two of his fullback teammates were coming in our direction. They took up the entire hallway. Ty was glowering, his look fixed on Dora like he wanted to tear her head off and kick it for a field goal. She laughed this surprisingly tinkly-sounding laugh and then she and her crew went in the other direction. Then the bell rang, which meant I was late. We were all late, since everyone around us had stopped to watch the show.

"Get to class, people," a teacher called out. "Now."

Ty slapped my chest. "Thanks, man." He still looked pissed. "We have a real cockroach problem in this school," he said loudly, so the retreating group would hear.

Dora tossed her hand in the air and flew him the bird.

"She really has a thing for you," I said to Ty.

"Yeah, I know." He looked over at Nikki. "You okay?"

She nodded and then looked at me. "Thank you."

"No prob," I said. "See you guys." As I continued on to Chemistry, it occurred to me that I didn't feel quite as irritable as I had. I even changed my mind about Valentine's Day a little bit when I walked into the cafeteria at lunch and saw Graylin sitting at our table. She'd spread out red napkins and set lunch out. Deli sandwiches, each cut into a heart shape, a bag of chips and a fat dill pickle wrapped in plastic wrap. I laughed. "What is this?" I asked as I sat.

"It is your Valentine's luncheon, my good sir."

It looked great. "Thanks," I said, setting my brown bag aside, generic PB & J already forgotten.

"I have something else for you, too," she said, reaching into her book bag. She brought up a clear, quart-sized baggie full of little envelopes, all with names on them. Written with a red sharpie, of course.

"Are those what I think they are?"

"Maybe." She found the one for me. On the envelope, it said, *And now your local sportscast with...*

I munched on my sandwich as I opened the card. On it was a cowgirl tossing a rope, and it bespoke of rustling me up as her valentine. "I accept."

"Awesome."

Ty sat beside me with a full lunch tray. "I'm jealous," he said, looking at our food.

"Oh, but I have a Valentine for you, too," Graylin replied. She fished in her bag.

I glanced over at Ty's normal lunch table and saw more than a few heads turned our way. They reminded me of puppies longing for their mama. "Where's Nikki?"

"She went home." He shoved a french fry in his mouth. "Those assholes really get to her."

Graylin made a face. "Not again."

"Again," he confirmed.

"Here," she said, handing a card over.

Ty grinned as he took it. "But I didn't get you anything, sweetheart."

"It's nothing you can't make up to me," she replied sweetly. "I wear a size four. I like Versace in evening wear. I prefer white gold in jewelry. *Hmm*, what else?"

Trust Graylin to turn a conversation around.

12

The next new guy. (Yeah. Awesome.)

The first week of March was filled with sixty-degree days. On Friday the 7th, it was due to hit seventy. My kind of weather.

"Matthews," Ty bellowed to me in the hallway in between third and fourth block. "Soccer game after school," he said when he reached me. "You're playing."

"Am I?"

"It's arranged. I'm kinda' like your agent."

"I'm flattered."

"You can play, right? Cause I'm going to look really stupid if you suck."

"It's been awhile, but I think I can probably hold my own."

"Good. A lot of the guys from the team will be there and if you're going to join them next year, you probably ought to meet them. Most of them are pretty cool." He looked around to make sure the coast was clear. "Jay Fields is a real douche bag," he said under his breath. "He's convinced he's God's gift to the game." He shrugged. "He doesn't suck, but I've seen better. You got clothes to change into or you want to run home after school?"

"I'll run home."

"Meet me out back and I'll drive you. I don't want them to start without us." He started to walk off.

"Are you playing, too?"

"Hell, yeah. Occasionally, I like to show them how it's done." He smirked and hurried on, almost colliding with Morgan. "Hey," he said to her. "Unofficial soccer game after school. You should show."

She shrugged, not terribly interested. "Maybe."

"Maybe, she says," Ty said to me. He rolled his eyes and went on his way.

I suddenly noticed people looking at me with … was that actually *admiration* in their eyes? Seriously? Ty was a good athlete, the star running back of our team, and he'd landed an athletic scholarship, a full friggin' ride, to Carolina. Which was great for him, but it didn't make him a candidate for the cover of Sports Illustrated. At least, not yet. And people were looking at me differently because we'd sort of become friends? It was a weird feeling, part flattering, but a little bit insulting, too.

The rest of the day flew by and then Ty drove me back to the apartment where I changed clothes as quickly as I could, which was less than two minutes since I hadn't tied even my shoes when I hobbled back to his car.

He looked at me with a wry expression. "You might want to tie your shoes there, Poncho. You look of kind of stupid."

"Poncho?"

He laughed and then drove entirely too fast. When we walked out to the field, most the guys were standing around talking. Maybe it was ridiculous to be nervous, but I was. I hadn't done any joining in a long time, outside of the Pleasantville study group that day.

"I hear your Ty's new bitch," a blonde guy said to me. I was pretty sure he was Jay Fields.

Ty cleared his throat, halfway camouflaging the word, "dick."

A few of the guys laughed. I'm not sure if they were laughing at Fields or if Ty's comment had come through.

"You suck his cock in between classes?" Fields asked.

For a second, it felt like I was in middle school again. I'd been frozen out of the team in seventh grade with similar bullshit.

"No, sweetheart," Ty said to Fields, before I could come up with a response. "Don't be jealous. I told him that was your job."

Field's smile turned sickly, but the other guys laughed their asses off.

"Yeah, it was a blow," I said to Fields. "That's a blow, not a blowjob."

More howls of laughter.

"A real fucking comedian, huh?" Fields said hotly as he stalked off. "Let's just see how long you laugh."

Ty shrugged. "Think we're going to have to file that one under 'can dish it out but cannot take it.'"

The game turned out to be intense, but I kept up just fine, scoring two goals and a dozen high fives. It felt great. It was funny, the better I did, the more pissed off Jay Fields became which really messed with his game. I'm pretty sure there's a worthy moral lesson in there. After the game, Ty invited me over for dinner. "Meatloaf," he said meaningfully. "Let me tell you, my Mom's meatloaf—" he kissed the tips of his fingers like a lusty Italian.

"Sounds good," I said. And it did.

As I pulled out my cell to run it by Mom, Ty sunk the final nail in the casket of Jay Field's bullshit. "Hey, Jay," he called with an exaggerated effeminate voice. "Want to come over for dinner? I'm feeling kind of horny, and Nikki has something going on tonight."

Fields flipped him off.

"Oh, wow," Ty said. "You're saying fuck you? Are we taking it there? I mean, that's like a serious step in our relationship, man."

"Hey, Larkin," Fields said angrily, "enough, already! It's not funny."

Ty just laughed. So did most of us. I kinda' doubt Fields will call me Ty's bitch again.

Mom answered the phone.

"Hey," I said, feeling on top of the world. "I'm going to a friend's house for dinner. Okay?"

"Uh, no, because there's someone here I want you to meet."

I felt a sick weight in the pit of my stomach. "Someone *where?*"

"We're home," she chirped.

The sick feeling intensified. "Come on, Mom. Does it have to be now?"

"Yeah. We have food, anyway."

I didn't reply for a moment, because I was trying to come up with a good argument for not going home to meet the newest guy. It was such a waste of my life and, for once, I actually had something else to do.

"Don't give me any shit," she said testily. "Okay?"

"Yeah, okay," I replied coldly. I closed my phone.

"What's wrong?" Ty asked.

"Nothing. I just gotta' go home."

He shrugged. "It's cool."

But it wasn't. I knew in my gut, it wasn't.

"This is Dave Reynolds," Mom said proudly as she wrapped her hands around his arm.

Great, I thought. Add a new name to the list.

"Dave, this is Matt."

"Hey, Matt."

"Hi." He looked like an average Joe, blue collar, probably mid-thirties, thinning hair, clean t-shirt and jeans. He wasn't bad looking, but he had the sort of face that would be hard to describe an hour after you'd met him.

"Dave got us Chinese for dinner," Mom said with a bright smile. It's her new guy smile. I gave it a lifespan of three weeks, tops.

"Hope you like it," Dave said to me.

"I do. Thanks."

A moment of supremely awkward silence ensued.

"I'll just go wash my hands," I said.

"Was it a good game?" Dave asked.

"I had a good time. Yeah. It was just for fun."

"I played a little in high school. Baseball was more my game, though."

I nodded. We all endured another moment of polite silence and then I made a gesture, indicating I was going to walk off and I did. Yeah. Stupid. Maybe it's awful, but it felt so good to walk away from them. I shut myself in the bathroom, turned the hot water tap on and looked into the mirror as I waited for the water to get warm. I won't claim that a stranger peered back at me, but I had become a lot more self-aware over the last few weeks. I'd also had a lot of fun that day. I'd felt a part of something normal for once in my life.

Dinner was good. It wasn't Tina Larkin's meatloaf, but it was way better fare than I usually have. Afterwards, I thanked Dave again and exiled myself to my room under the pretense of homework. I was stretched out on my bed listening to my IPod when Mom opened my door a few hours later. I pulled the earphones out of my ears.

"Did you finish your homework?" she asked.

I think I scowled and I know I didn't answer, because I seriously cannot remember how many years it's been since she asked that, if she ever asked. The sheer freaking pretense was irritating. What was she doing? Playing the part of the doting mother? Was she going to ask me if I'd brushed my teeth next?

She took a few steps in. "He's an aircraft mechanic."

I felt a twinge of nerves. "Yeah, I heard." She sat on the edge of my bed, obviously wanting to say something. The twinge suddenly became a sharp, warning pain in my stomach. I sat up, alarmed. "Oh, no. No way."

Her eyes widened. "What?"

This was going to be about moving. I knew that look on her face. "I've only got one year of high school to go," I said as calmly as I was capable. "And I've just started to fit in. For the first time! Anywhere."

"Matt."

"No, don't Matt me. I've never asked you for anything. Not one fucking thing. But I want to stay here next year."

"We'd only be going to Charlotte. It's not even two hours away."

"You just met this guy," I practically yelled.

"No, *you* just met him. I've been seeing him for a while."

"What's a while, Mom? Two weeks? I'll bet you anything it hasn't been more than two weeks. And it won't last. And, for that, you'd tear up my life? Again?"

She huffed and stood. "I'm sorry you feel that way about it."

"No, you're not. You don't give a shit. You don't give a shit about anybody but yourself!"

"What the hell's gotten into you? You don't talk this way."

"I'm sick of it! I swear, if you make me move again, I will never forgive you."

She opened her mouth to speak, but then shut it again. Livid, she turned and started from the room, and I shoved my earphones back in and cranked up the music so I wouldn't have to hear another word she said.

I turned onto my side, feeling embarrassingly close to tears. It wasn't just self-pity, I was pissed. It wasn't right. It wasn't fair, and I probably wouldn't be able to do a damn thing about it. After a few minutes of pressure building, I yanked my earphones, got up and shadow boxed my opponent to a pulp. I was *sick* of feeling out of control of my own life. I stopped, closed my eyes and beckoned for Sirena with all the mental might I possessed.

I felt the calming of her presence before I felt her press herself against my back and wrap her arms around me. Sighing with relief, my eyes still closed, I reached up and covered her hands with my own, and she clasped and intertwined her fingers with mine. It felt so good with her pressed against me. My body reacted, I wanted more, and then I made the mistake. I opened my eyes and started to turn, only she wasn't there. For a second, I hated myself. I hated my impatience. Why hadn't I just kept my eyes shut?

Still, she'd felt my need and she'd come to me and that was something.

It was a lifeline.

.

13

Outcasts, unite!

For more than a week in mid-march, Graylin didn't come to school. We texted and played phone tag, but her messages were brief and not very revealing. I missed her, but I started joining Ty's lunch table. It's probably going to sound stupid, but it felt like a big step for me because, so far, my social encounters had been either accidental or somebody else's doing. I hadn't done the joining. I guess, subconsciously, I was thinking that if everything fell apart, at least, I hadn't put myself out there all the way.

Anyway, I had a couple of interesting realizations that week. First, it's not just different being part of group, it's *completely* different. When you're alone, all this effort goes into maintaining this wall, this humiliation barrier, around you. Sure, you notice things and people beyond it, but you don't want to appear to. You feel alone, set apart, but you don't want to seem like it, so you concentrate on whatever you're reading or writing or eating and you try not to notice how people look and/or talk about you. But when you're part of group, you don't think about any of that. You're caught up in what's happening or what's being said at the moment. It's not the opposite experience; it's a totally alternate experience.

Somewhere along the line, I don't even know when, I'd stopped fearing I was going to be frozen out and just started being. Not that I still don't feel like the outsider, because I do. I don't think that's ever going away completely. It's been part of who I am for so long, it's encoded itself onto my DNA.

The fact is, I keep most of my thoughts to myself. Obviously, I would never talk about my trances or visitations to Ruaun3, and I can't talk about the brat squad. I also hadn't mentioned moving to anyone. Mostly, because I was pretending the possibility didn't exist. Mom has a really short attention span where men are concerned, so the Dave thing might just blow over. Nothing against Dave, he seems like a good guy.

I really can't remember what we talked about that Friday at lunch, not until a girl at our table named Beth Anne said, "Slut alert."

"Don't do that," Nikki retorted, flushing angrily.

I guess it was morbid curiosity that made me look over as a girl, I assumed Suzanne Farlow, walked by with a lunch tray. She was kind of plain, but not unattractive with a mass of long brown hair that was pulled back in a big clip. I think she may have heard Beth Anne, because she glanced over at our table. I looked in the opposite direction, ashamed to have been caught staring, and that's when I noticed the expressions on Beth Anne and Morgan's face, the amusement and smug superiority. It made me feel sick to my stomach because I'd been on the opposite end of that sort of look too many times. When the populars target you and freeze you out, that's the look you get afterwards. And the thing is, it's contagious.

I got up and took my tray to return it. Nikki came right behind me and dumped the contents of her tray, then stacked it in the bin. "You ever want to do something about it?" I asked her.

She looked at me and her eyes filled.

I felt like a jerk. I hadn't been trying to make her feel guilty. I mean, if there was anybody who didn't need to feel guilty, it was her. "Sorry."

"No, it's okay."

"No. I shouldn't have said anything."

"No, Matt, it's okay. I get it. I do. I'm just going to get—" She bobbed her head toward the cafeteria line.

I nodded and started back to the table feeling totally out of my league. It hadn't been all that long since I'd been introduced into society, and I wasn't always what you might call smooth at social discourse. Yeah, okay. That is a vast understatement.

I could have sat right back down at the place I'd vacated. Ty was holding court, as usual, making everyone laugh. It would have been easy enough, but I couldn't go from being a lone wolf to being part of a group mentally abusing the most recent outcast. Suzanne, if that's who she was, was sitting alone, of course, and some of the kids around her were being jerks. I walked over and stood at the end of the table, next to her. "Mind if I sit down?"

She looked up at me and then glanced around and then looked back at her plate, as if it might hold a clue to serious global issues. "It's a free country," she mumbled.

I sat, completely aware of the stares and laughter. I hoped to God I just hadn't made a shitty situation worse.

She stabbed her fork at a chef salad that should have made chefs everywhere cringe. It was comprised of pale iceberg lettuce, thinly sliced eggs, tomatoes and ham, all of which looked as if they had seen better days. "Just so you know," she said, "I don't date anymore and I'm out of the porn business."

"Aren't you kind of young to be in the porn business, much less to be at the point of retiring?"

She looked up at me, not sure what to make of the statement.

"I'm Matt."

"I know who you are. Why are you sitting here?"

I hesitated a moment, and then shrugged. "I thought this was one the outcast's table."

For a second, she looked totally taken aback. "That's about right. I sat here today, so now it's the big, fat loser's table."

"I said outcast. Not big, fat loser."

"Same thing," she said as she went back to stabbing at her salad. "Why would you be here, anyway? I mean, if this were the outcasts' table."

I blew out a breath. "How long you got?"

She peeked up at me. "I don't know. Every lunch period from now until the end of school, I guess."

I pursed my lips and nodded slowly. "Not sure that's quite enough time, but I guess we could get started."

She studied a few moments to determine if I was serious or not. "You know who I am, right?"

"Suzanne?"

"You know what I mean," she said quietly.

"Yeah, I know what you mean. Yes, I heard about it. Everyone's heard about it. You know, the world keeps on turning. There have been a few other natural catastrophes since yours."

She smirked. "That's a first."

Nikki stopped at our table with a carton of chocolate pudding and a plastic spoon. "Can I join ya'll?"

"Good by me," I said.

Suzanne nodded. She was turning red.

Nikki sat next to me. "Uh, Suzanne, that's like the worst looking salad ever. And I do mean ever."

"I know," Suzanne agreed, stabbing it again. "It tastes as bad as it looks, too." She suddenly looked at Nikki. "This isn't a joke, is it?"

"Oh, my God! I wouldn't do that."

Suzanne nodded, apparently believing it. "Sorry."

"No," Nikki replied regretfully. "I've wanted to say something. I'm really sorry for what happened to you."

"It didn't just happen," Suzanne corrected. "I was stupid." She looked at me.

"No argument here," I said quietly.

"But it shouldn't have played out like it did," Nikki rejoined.

Suzanne speared a thin slice of egg and ate it and Nikki opened her pudding and stirred. I wished I had some food to play with, too. "So, what was the last embarrassing or really stupid thing you did?" I asked Nikki.

She blushed and bit on her bottom lip. "Oh, I don't know."

"Come on," I laughingly coaxed. "I can tell you just thought of something."

She looked at Suzanne and then me. "Swear you won't tell anyone."

"I swear," I pledged.

Nikki looked at Suzanne, who nodded manically and parroted, "Swear."

Nikki sighed. "My brother, he's a year younger than me, had a friend over and we were all in the kitchen, talking and eating after school." She paused and looked pained.

"Yeah," I encouraged. "And?"

"I realized I had to, uh, you know … I felt a little wind," she said, whispering the last word.

We chuckled, and I felt a cursed heat of a blush.

Her cheeks also glowed. "I went out to get the mail, so that I could—" she gestured.

We nodded, barely holding back a peel of obnoxious laughter.

"I could have just gone to the bathroom and turned on the fan and the water, but I did need to get the mail, so I went outside and—"

"Yeah, yeah. Been there, done that," I spoke up to help her out when she paused.

"Really?" she asked shyly.

"Of course. Everyone has."

"Only it was louder than I'd thought," she admitted.

Now we couldn't help laughing.

"A little bit louder … like a trumpet?" I suggested making Suzanne laugh even harder.

Nikki was nodding, although she looked like she was in great pain. "It would have been no big deal; except my next-door neighbor and two other men I've never seen before were standing like ten yards away." She shook her head. "I thought I was going to die!"

Nikki had to wait for our laughing fit to end before she added, "You swore."

"I'll take it to my grave," I said.

"Me, too," Suzanne echoed.

"What about you?" Nikki challenged me. "And you'd better have one!"

I thought about it. "I don't have anything that funny but, not very long ago, this girl, Graylin Hall," I looked at Suzanne. "Do you know her?"

Suzanne nodded. "She's great," she said. "When everything happened, she—" her eyes filled and she looked away for a second. "She's great," she repeated in a thick voice.

It's probably dumb, but I felt so proud of Graylin at that moment. She doesn't just talk the talk. She actually walks the walk. I really hope we stay friends for the rest of our lives. "Well, this one day, she sits down across from me, right over there where I was being my normal hermit self. She'd made up her mind she wanted to be friends, but I was used to not having any, so I tried to blow her off."

"I don't get it," Nikki said. "Why?"

I shrugged. "You have a few bad experiences. Kids being rotten to you, and you close down the possible avenues of it happening again."

"When did that happen to you?" Nikki asked with an aggrieved expression

"Middle school, mostly. Seventh grade. Eighth grade. Don't ask me why, but I became the mark for this one group of guys. They made my life a living hell."

"I'm sorry," Nikki said.

"Me, too," Suzanne added.

"Me, three. But, looking back, I wish I hadn't let it do the damage it did. Even once we moved and life might have been a whole different thing, I stayed shut off. I didn't give anyone or anything a chance." Looking at Suzanne, I added, "You shouldn't let the assholes win. You know?"

She nodded and then she looked at Nikki. "I'm so sorry about what happened to Madison. I would have gone to the funeral, but—"

Nikki nodded. "It was crowded," she said in a thick voice. "The church couldn't hold everyone."

"It's because she was so liked," Suzanne said.

Nikki nodded again.

"Are you okay?" Suzanne asked. "You've lost weight."

"I'm not okay, exactly, but I know I will be. Some day. Going away to school will help."

"I know what you mean," Suzanne said. "I'm going to move in with my dad this summer. He lives in Connecticut."

"Hey," Beth Anne chirped, having walked over.

We all jerked a little, because we'd been so into the conversation, we hadn't seen her approach.

"Looks like the party's shifted over here," Beth Anne said. "Mind if I join?"

"I do," Suzanne stated clearly, her eyes blazing with hatred.

Beth Anne made a soft grunt and looked around, her face turning as red as Suzanne's had been earlier. "Whatever," she said. "I might have gotten a disease, anyway." She walked back off.

"She's such a bitch," Suzanne fumed under her breath.

"Like I said," I spoke up. "Here's to not letting the assholes win."

Suzanne reached for her glass and raised it. "I'll drink to that."

Ty suddenly shoved in next to Suzanne. "You going to eat that pudding or pass it to me?" he asked Nikki.

"Obviously, I'm going to eat it."

"It doesn't look obvious to me. You've hardly taken a bite."

Nikki dug in and took a big bite. Like half the carton.

"Whatever," he laughed. "Whassup Zannie," Ty asked, bumping into her.

Suzanne pushed back. The smile on her face said a lot about Ty, I thought.

When the bell rung, Ty followed me. "Hey, I got a nickname for you," he said confidentially.

"What's that?"

"You've heard of Mother Teresa?"

I almost laughed. I could feel what was coming. "Once or twice, yeah."

"From henceforth, you shall be known as Mother Matt. Mother Matthew Matthews, with a heart of gold, ministering to the needy and the forlorn," he said in an affected voice.

I had to laugh.

"We'll call you Triple M, for short," he said walking off with a big grin on his face. "My man, Triple M," he called. Then he howled.

14

Hannah's Hardware

After school, I went to work. It's about a twenty-minute walk from school, but Morgan saw me walking and offered me a ride and I accepted.

"Are you mad at me?" she asked on the way.

I was surprised by the question. "No."

"I mean, you left the table and went over and sat with Su—zanne."

I shrugged. "Yeah."

"You know about her, right?"

"Yeah, I heard the story." I almost stopped there, but then I added, "Personally, I think it sucks how she's being treated. Like she's a leper."

"Well, she did it to herself. Took pictures of—"

"I heard."

"You heard or you saw?" she asked coyly.

"Morgan, no offense, but I'm kind of done with the conversation. Okay?"

"Okay. I just don't want you to be mad at me. Actually, what I really wanted was to tell you was—"

"What?"

"You can't say anything or even let on."

This was going to be about Steph. "Okay."

"Steph likes you. I know you're going out with Graylin Hall, and she is really cute." She paused and I thought about jumping in and telling her I wasn't dating Graylin, but I didn't. "But if it doesn't work out, Steph is terrific."

"She seems terrific," I stammered.

"You can't say anything. She'd be so pissed at me."

"I won't."

She nodded, satisfied. "I heard Beth Anne totally got frozen out. That is hilarious."

Said one vulture about the other. I continued looking out the window.

"What were you guys talking about? You were laughing like crazy."

"Don't really remember," I said, not even trying to make it sound believable.

"Well, here we are," she said as we pulled in front of the store.

I couldn't get out quickly enough. "Thanks for the ride."

"Anytime."

When I stepped inside the front door of Hannah's Hardware, Toby was giggling. "I saw that girl," he said.

"She's just a friend, Tob," I replied as I went for my work apron.

"Sure," Toby said, stretching out the word.

"Not that I don't have lots of girlfriends, because obviously I do, but she's not one of them."

Toby was delighted.

A couple of hours later, I was in the back room organizing cans of paint from a new shipment when Ev stuck his head in the door. "Oh, Matthew?"

He never calls me Matthew. "Yes, Everett Hannah the fourth?"

He chuckled. "There's an awful pretty young lady here to see you."

I frowned, wondering if it was Morgan again. Or Steph. I hoped not.

"Been holding out on us, I think," Ev remarked with a smirk.

"Hardly," I replied. I walked past him and saw Graylin standing at the front counter talking to Toby. What a relief. She was perfectly calm, but her blue eyes blazed with excitement. I was *so* glad to see her.

"Hey. What time's your break?" she asked when I reached her.

"Right now," Ev said behind me, slapping my shoulder.

I don't really get official breaks, because we're just not that official at the store. I looked back at Ev. "I won't be long."

"Go, go," Ev waved me off.

Toby was dancing foot to foot, barely stifling a giggle.

I followed Graylin but double stepped around her in order to open the door for her.

"How did you ever become such a gentleman in this day and age?"

"I guess it's instinctual."

She chortled. "Trust me when I tell you it's not." She walked to her car and leaned against it looking like that cat that ate the canary.

"What's going on?" I asked.

"We got one of them. A guy named Troy Baylor tried to grab Charlie this morning."

My heart did a painful double flip in my chest.

"She's okay," Graylin assured me. "Baylor tried to nab her, but our guys were on him like white on rice."

I went and leaned against her car, too. It shook me that someone had gone after Charlie. What if no one had been watching her? What if he'd gotten her? I thought of the other victims and shuddered at the thought of a repeat. "What happened?"

Graylin turned to me. "This morning, Charlie got off the bus and started toward the front doors like every day, but then she turned. Like someone had called her name. So all the other kids are going this way, but Charlie's going this way. Caleb and Frank jumped out of the car and closed in from either side. By then, Charlie was talking to Baylor. He had a bag in his hand that he claimed Ty sent for her. He went to grab her, but Frank took him down."

"Oh, man. That must have scared her."

"Yeah, it did. She went home after."

"I bet."

"You'd think right there in front of school, there is no way it can happen, but Baylor found this little blind spot."

"Weren't teachers around?"

She nodded. "They were. The usual one or two, but they didn't see it."

"So, what did Baylor say when you took him in. Or can't you tell me?"

"He isn't talking, but guess whose picture he has in his wallet?"

I grimaced. "Dora?"

She nodded. "Dora Blake, aka Skunk girl."

Goosebumps covered the entire surface of my skin.

"Baylor is nineteen. He's looking at serious time but, so far, he's protecting her."

"You really think Dora was behind it?" I asked. "Couldn't it be the other way around?"

"Oh, she's behind it. Baylor has her initials tattooed on his chest."

"Skunk girl?" I asked woefully.

"I don't get it either." She paused. "Hey, Matt?"

"Yeah?"

"I'm not officially telling you this or anything, but we only knew about Charlie because of you. She's safe because of you. Everybody played their part, but we wouldn't have known to watch her. You should feel really good about that, Sherlock. Seriously."

Wow. The statement rendered me speechless. It was surprising, make that shocking, and it proof, too. Proof that whatever was happening with me was real. The trances, Sirena, Ruaun3, all of it. "Thanks."

"From now on, a teacher will be posted at that blind spot when kids are going or coming. Good stuff, all." She reached over and tugged by sleeve then stepped back. "I've got to get back and you have some explaining to do."

Yep, Toby was watching us with sheer delight. I grinned. "I guess I do."

"You're such a good guy. If only you were a little older."

"Uh, emotionally, I'm like thirty-five, and you're still, like, eighteen. Remember? I'll graduate from high school next year and you might not for years to come."

"That almost makes you sound like an old perv."

"Yeah, well." I shrugged and then went around and opened her car door for her. "I should tell you, some people think we're dating. I never said so, but I … may have allowed them think so."

"Works for me," she said with a shrug. "Gotta protect the cover." She climbed in, and I shut the door for her. We waved and then each of us went back to work.

The next day, Ev and I were in the back room finishing inventory. I had a pencil gripped in my teeth as I counted boxes of standard 60-watt light bulbs. I'm glad we only conduct inventory twice a year, because it's as boring as it is time consuming. Imagine the thrill of counting plungers and hammers. Tarps and rakes. Bags of grass seed and weed killer. Just listing the stuff makes me want to doze.

"Where's all the paint thinner gone?" Ev muttered. "You sell a bunch of paint thinner lately?"

I took the pencil from my teeth and jotted the number of light bulbs on my sheet. "Nope."

"Hey, Toby," Ev called.

Toby rushed in a minute later. "Yeah, Daddy?"

"Have you sold a bunch of paint thinner lately?"

Toby nodded. "Yes, sir."

"How much?"

"All we had."

"To how many people?"

"One."

I looked at Ev as he looked at me. "Who buys that much paint thinner?" he asked hesitantly.

"He was kind of weird. He had all black hair, except for a braid."

My eyes bulged. "Was the braid white?"

"Yeah. He had makeup on his eyes, too."

Ev glanced at me, then looked back at Toby. "How much did he buy?"

Toby looked toward the ceiling and counted on his fingers as he thought about it. "Two cases and four more cans."

A chill crept up my spine. "What else did he buy?"

"*Um*, nails and a soda and a package of Starbursts." He shifted on his feet nervously. "Did I do something wrong?"

"No, you didn't do anything wrong," Ev replied. "It's just strange, him buying that much paint thinner. That's all. Struck me as odd. Tell you what, though, when someone wants to buy that much of anything, why don't you tell me about it first? Or Matt. And then we'll ask some questions, maybe take a name."

"Okay."

"How many nails?" I asked, trying to keep my voice calm and even.

"Six boxes. The big boxes, not the little ones."

"Did he pay with a credit card?" I asked.

He shook his head. "He paid with cash. He got seventy-two cents back. I thought he had a lot of painting to do. I said so and he said that was right."

"Okay," Ev said. "You can go back out front now."

"I'm hungry," Toby said. "Can we get lunch soon?"

"Yeah, I'm hungry, too," Ev replied. "I'm going to the diner today."

Toby lit up. "Can I have a reuben?"

"Sure you can. I'll get us all a reuben."

"I'll go get some money from the register," Toby declared, hurrying back out.

Ev turned to me, concerned. "You know who the guy was?"

"I think so. There's this group at school that wear that hair like that, black and white."

"Think they're up to no good?"

"I think they're all pretty much no good."

Ev rubbed the back of his neck. "Tell you what, I'm going to get us some lunch and then we'll decide if we should call the cops. I don't know that they'll take it real seriously is the only thing. After all, it's just paint thinner." He paused. "And nails."

"I know somebody we can report it to," I offered.

His eyes widened. "Yeah?"

"Yeah. It's somebody that works ... security at school. In fact, this person's in law enforcement."

Ev looked hopeful. "You mind doing that?"

"No, of course not. It may be nothing, but—"

"Yeah, *but*. In this day and time. You know?"

I nodded.

"Okay," he said. "Good. That makes me feel better." He started for the door. "I'll go for lunch and be back in ten. Unless they're crowded. A Rueben okay with you?"

"Yes, sir. That'd be great."

As Ev left, I was super edgy. I went to the last few rows to be inventoried looking for the bags of manure. There was only one bag left, but I was pretty sure there had been more. When had I last seen it? I walked out front. "Hey, Toby, when did you sell the paint thinner?"

"This morning, when we first opened."

"Oh, yeah? And you said the guy claimed he had a lot of painting to do?"

"Yeah. He said he was helping to paint some buildings red."

My throat closed and goosebumps broke out all over me.

"You okay, Matt?"

"Yeah, sure," I said automatically. "Did you sell any manure lately?"

Toby gawked. "How did you know? The guy with the braid? His friend bought eight bags."

I started nodding before I realized it and stopped myself. "Did his friend look weird, too?"

"Yeah. His hair was white, and his ponytail was black."

"I've seen them at school," I said.

"They weren't very nice. They were laughing at me."

"They're *not* nice, Toby. And they're not worth thinking about. I'm going to step out and make a phone call. Okay?"

"Okay."

I walked and called Graylin. I got her voice mail and almost hung up but, at the last second, I changed my mind. "It's Matt," I said after the beep. "It may be nothing, but a couple members of the skunk club bought a bunch of paint thinner, manure and nails this morning. They told Toby they were going to paint some buildings red." Saying it out loud – it didn't feel like I was making something out of nothing. It seemed like something. "I don't know. I've got a bad feeling."

She called back not even two minutes later. "We're on it," she said grimly. "I'll call you later."

Seven words, five seconds, and it felt like a huge weight had been lifted off my shoulders and chest. When Ev got back with lunch, I told him as much I could, which was enough to relieve his mind. The rest of the day was uneventful, if you don't count the little jig I performed in private when inventory was done.

When I locked up to go home, I found Graylin outside, waiting for me. "You could have come in," I told her.

"I just got here and, besides, I haven't had a second to myself all day. You want to take a ride?"

"Sure. What's going on?"

"Stuff," she said meaningfully. "You need to call your mom or anything?"

"Nah. She won't be home."

Graylin's looked at me, her expression curious.

"Let's just say she does the best she can, but she's never going to be nominated for mother of the year."

"Gotcha."

We got in the car and she drove. "Where are we going?"

"To watch some interviews if you want." She pulled into the diner just down the street, the one that Ev always goes to for lunch. "After we eat. I'm starved."

At Jerry and Lou's Diner, circa 1950, the only thing that's changed since 1950 is that most of the drive-in stations were removed. Two are left, either for the purpose of nostalgia or because renovation funds dried up. The place has character.

Plus, they make great reubens and the absolute best onion rings ever. "What interviews?" I asked as we walked in.

"Let's order and then I'll tell you."

The diner was nearly empty. It was just after seven, but the patrons of Jerry & Lou's are early birds. The bulk of the clientele is over sixty and the dinner rush is around five-thirty. We slid into a booth and looked over the menu, although the special of country-fried steak, mashed potatoes and green beans already had my vote. Served with your choice of a corn muffin or a homemade buttermilk biscuit, it's soul food with enough carbs to fuel a hike up Mount Kilimanjaro.

"This place is wild," Graylin said, looking around. "They need to move it lock, stock and barrel to the Smithsonian."

"After replacing all the drive-in stations," I added.

"And there needs to be a radio station blasting hits by Elvis and Jerry Lee Lewis. I just picture the waitresses on roller-skates."

"Ya'll ready?" asked an aging waitress in a fuchsia uniform and perfectly matching lipstick. Her nametag said Phyllia. I wondered if it was an old family name or if the nametag company misread a request for Phyllis.

"Yes, ma'am," Graylin replied. "I'd like The Big Bop plate with onion rings, please."

"All-righty," the lady said as she scribbled on the order pad.

"And a limeade," Graylin added.

"Got it." The waitress looked at me. "And you, sweetheart?"

"I'll have the special please."

"Cornbread or a biscuit?"

"Surprise me. I like them both."

"Then I'll bring 'em both. And to drink?"

"Water's fine."

"Oh, have a limeade, too," Graylin said. "I mean, how often do you get to order one?"

I caved. "And a limeade." I usually order water because any other beverage adds at least a dollar to the bill. I'm poor, not cheap, mind you; not that the distinction makes much of a difference.

"You got it," Phyllia replied.

"The bill is mine, by the way," Graylin told the waitress.

"All-righty, sweetheart. And ya'll save some room for dessert. We got fresh coconut cream pie that is to die for."

"Yum," Graylin said enthusiastically. "We'll take it. And coffee." She cocked her head at me. "Do you drink coffee?"

"Not much," I said, feeling like a kid.

"One coffee, then."

"Decaf?" the waitress asked.

"No," Graylin exclaimed as if the suggestion horrified her.

"Honey, that is how I feel about it, too," Phyllia agreed. "Don't see the point in unleaded coffee or alcohol-free beer myself."

Graylin nodded. "I'm with you."

"Thanks," I said to Graylin when Phyllia walked off. "This is a treat."

"Are you kidding? We so owe you."

"What's happened?"

"You ready to hear it?" she teased. "I mean, we could kick back, relax and eat first."

"I could also kick you under the table."

She grinned and leaned forward. "After we talked, we sent unies to other hardware stores and drug stores to see if there had been other big purchases of potentially explosive material."

"Unies?"

"Uniforms. Cops."

I nodded.

"We got search warrants and visited the residences of Ben Fisher, aka Fish, Dustin Pegram, also known as Dust, Luke Summers, aka BB—"

"BB?"

She shrugged. "No idea where he got the nickname yet."

"So, what did they find?"

"In the Pegram basement, the cops found a lab of sorts. For making bombs."

"Oh, man," I breathed. I'd thought it was possible, but to hear it stated as fact was sickening.

"Dust lives with his grandmother, this clueless old lady who can't even get up and down the steps anymore. She had no idea what was going on in the basement. She thought he was building model cars. The bomb squad is still over there dismantling."

"Seriously?"

"Yes. There were enough ingredients to blow up half the schools in the district, although they hadn't put that much together yet."

I recalled the carnage I'd seen in my trance and a painful shiver racked me. "You think that's what they were going to do?"

"We found maps of four high schools, including North. We also found recipes for TATP." She stopped talking as Phyllia approached with our drinks. "Thanks."

"Sure thing," Phillia returned.

"What's TATP?" I asked when we were alone again.

"It's short for triacetone triperoxide. Basically, it's what makes bombs blow up. What's interesting is that the recipes were downloaded from the Internet only last night. We think when Troy Baylor got picked up, plan B went into play."

"Plan B was to blow up schools?"

She nodded. "Paint them red."

The words were sickening, and I could only stare. What a stroke of blind luck it had been! What if we hadn't taken inventory that day? What if Ev hadn't remarked about the paint thinner? That hadn't been skill or detective work on my part, or even a nudge from my psylink, it had been luck. "If Ev hadn't noticed the paint thinner," I said.

"I know. Scary. So is the fact that Eudora Blake is MIA."

Eudora. "Did you get all the others?"

"We hope so. They hadn't said a word when I left, but maybe they'll be talking by the time we get back."

"I really get to go with you?"

She grinned mischievously. "We've got it figured out."

Our food was served and we dug in. A euphoria had come over me, not only because of the delicious food, but because the carnage I'd seen in my trance had been from bombs that wouldn't go off now. No one would ever know the senseless tragedy that had been averted, which was fine by me. Perfect, even, for someone who was invisible. No, for someone who had *thought* himself to be invisible. I wasn't feeling invisible anymore.

The death of Mister Invisible. A good title. In fact, what a phenomenal essay I could write now. The only problem is, who'd ever believe it?

15

The confession

Laura met us in the parking lot, and it was her that led me into the SBI squad room while Graylin hung back. The euphoria I'd felt earlier had evaporated and been replaced with nerves. Laura walked with me to an observation room. "This'll be Troy Wayne Baylor," she said before we stepped inside. It was crowded, but no one noticed us. They were focused on the interview in the adjoining interrogation room watched through a one-way mirror.

Besides Troy Baylor, whom I'd never seen before, there were two men in suits. Baylor was a short, stocky guy with deeply set eyes and a buzz cut.

"You should think about that," one of the men said to Baylor. "If one of the others do the talking, they get the break."

"Wah, wah, wah," Troy uttered with a deadpan expression.

"When you're the one who most needs it. You could be looking at a life sentence. Or worse. Depends on how you look at it. And on what we learn."

Baylor couldn't have looked more bored. "Wah, wah, wah."

I looked over at Laura questioningly, and she leaned close. "Earlier, he was doing that little hand gesture," she whispered. "Like a hand puppet talking. Maybe his arm got tired."

"Has he said anything else?" I whispered back.

She shook her head.

The door opened. It was Caleb who snapped his fingers a couple of times and gestured for us to come. At least a third of the room cleared out, including us, trailing along in back. I was pretty sure I had been snuck in without Randy's knowledge.

"Summers is talking," Caleb explained as we went toward another interrogation room. "His uncle, who is also his guardian, asked for a minute alone with him and slapped the shit out of him. Seems to have worked."

We entered the room and filed in to stand next to Graylin. I recognized Luke Summers from school, although now he was crying. His face was red, his nose dripping snot. There were two other men in the room, the uncle and an agent. The uncle was in a stained t-shirt and poorly fitting jeans. The agent looked like what one would expect an agent to look like. Dark suit and tie, a level gaze.

The agent reached for a box of tissues and slid it to Luke. "Explain why Dora fixated on Kaci Smith."

"They w-went to the same s-school," Luke stammered as he reached for the tissues and wiped his nose. "Dora went to West Washington last year," he said in a muffled voice. He blew his nose.

"Go on."

Luke took a deep breath and his shoulders quivered. "Okay, so Dora g-goes into the bathroom at school one day and Kaci and some of her friends were in there talking. About sh-shoes." He hiccupped.

"Shoes?"

"Yeah. Like fancy, designer shoes." He looked worn out. "Kaci was talking about a pair of shoes that had been, like, autographed. Dora said something about it 'cause she didn't get why someone would, like, autograph a shoe, and Kaci looked at her like she was dirt."

"So, Kaci just stared at her?" the agent coaxed.

"Well, no. I mean, she explained, but it was like she was talking to white trash."

"You're saying that's what Dora thought?"

He nodded. "Yeah. And something snapped in Dora. She said Kaci was going to die. She said the last thing the bitch would know is what it felt like to have *her* autograph."

The uncle cleared his throat. "Can we get something in writing about how he's cooperating and all?"

The agent looked at the older man. "As I explained, I will request some leniency for his cooperation but, first, I need to know what he knows." He looked back at Summers. "If you help us figure this whole mess out, you have my word that I'll do what I can for you. You're going to need a friend."

"The others'll hate me," Luke blubbered.

"Shut up," his uncle threatened under his breath. "Or so help me, God—"

"Go on," the agent interrupted. "You were telling me about Kaci."

Luke grabbed some more tissues and blew his nose again. "Dora followed her all last summer. She even got into her house a couple of times and looked around. She stole a shirt once. A lipstick another time. She still wears that lipstick. Says it her favorite shade."

I swallowed hard. Suddenly, dinner wasn't sitting so well.

"She's really good at B&E," Luke continued. "She can get in anywhere."

"The day of the murder," the agent asked. "How did that go down?"

"That was Dora, Dust and TW," he exclaimed. "I wasn't there. I swear it."

"What did you hear about it?"

"That Troy and Dust held Kaci and Dora ... did it."

"Be specific."

"Choked her to death."

"With what?"

"This cord thing. Dora made it."

"You've seen it?"

"Yeah. She usually has it on her."

The uncle shook his head. "You deserve to go away, you piece of shit."

"Mr. Summers, please," the agent snapped.

"I'm going to get some air," the old man grumbled. He got to his feet and lumbered from the room, limping slightly.

"When did you learn about Kaci's death?" the agent continued.

"The next day, I guess."

"You guess?"

"The next day. After it happened."

"What day was that?"

"It was a Saturday. I don't remember the date. It was in September."

"What was Dust's part in it?"

"He just helped hold Kaci down. And when she was almost dead, he cut the bottom of her foot."

I looked at Graylin. By her expression I saw that she already knew this bizarre fact.

"Why?" the agent pressed.

"Don't you get it? That was the autograph. Dora signed her foot."

"What was the signature?"

"It was an E."

The agent nodded.

"So, you know her real name?" Summers asked.

"Yes, BB, we do. So far, all you're doing is confirming what we already know. And possibly shaving off a little time off your sentence."

Summers lips quivered. "Don't call me BB."

There was a beat of silence. "I'm going to have you write out everything you recall about what was said in regard to Kaci. What time, location, how did they get in?"

"You know all that," Luke complained.

"I want to know what you were told and when. Now, tell me about the next victim? Ellyn Lamb?"

Summers sighed. "Dora hated her for same reason she hated Madison. Because everyone loved them. Because they had everything."

"How did she know Ellyn?"

"Don't you already know all this?"

"Are you finished cooperating?" the agent replied coldly.

The question seemed to rattle Luke. "The Lambs lived down the street from Dora's old group home," he continued. "The one she got kicked out of before the one she's in now. She didn't really *know* Ellyn, she just saw her. And watched her."

"Fixated on her?" the agent said.

"Shit, yes. Totally. She wanted to *be* her."

"And you were present for that murder?"

"No! I mean, yeah, but ... not for the actual *thing*. I didn't know what they were going to do!"

"Tell me."

"We were at the mall."

"Who?"

"Me, Dora, Dust and Dora's boyfriend, TW. For a while, we followed Ellyn, but I didn't think nothin' of it. I got bored. I wanted to go to the arcade, but she got all pissy about it. Said I had to stand guard on the door of this one bathroom. Tell anybody who tried to come in that it was out of order. Then she goes to the bathroom and me and TW follow her. He went inside after her, so I figured they were going to have sex." He paused. "No one came around and then TW motioned me in. I went in, I thought they might have a doobie to share, but ... she was there," he said with a haunted expression.

"Who was there?"

"Ellyn," Luke snapped. He looked ready to burst into tears again. "She was ... d-dead." He quivered and looked sick to his stomach.

"You're sure of that?"

"Hell, yeah, I'm sure. Her eyes were open. Her face was all swollen."

I blew a long, deep breath out. I needed to get out of there. I was just about to go when Graylin grabbed my hand in support. Or maybe because she needed it, although it was probably support. She seemed pretty stoic.

"Go on," the agent said.

"Man, I didn't know she was in there – and then there she is. Dead. Dora said it was time to prove I was one of them. She hands me this knife and tells me to cut an E into the bottom of Ellyn's foot." He huffed. "I said fuck no. No fucking way. But then TW said he'd slit my throat if I didn't and they'd make it look like I'd killed her."

The agent pulled back a chair and sat. "Go on."

"Why do I have to when you already know?" Luke whined.

The agent gave him a hard look.

Luke looked down and shook her head. "She had on sandals. Her toenails were painted different colors. I'll never forget that. But I did it. I mean, I had to. They were going to kill me if I didn't."

"So you removed her sandal?"

"Yes. They said I had to."

"And you cut an E on the bottom of her foot?"

Summers glared in aggravation. "Yeah, well, I meant to. I can't help it if I'm fucking dyslexic, can I? I mean, if I can concentrate … but I couldn't think straight."

"I don't doubt there was a lot of stress."

"Bet your ass there was. They've never stopped making fun of me for it, either. Call me Three and backwards boy."

BB. Backwards Boy.

"I didn't want to do it! I didn't even want to be there."

The agent observed Luke dispassionately for long moments. "Has it occurred to you that had you told anyone about what might happen to Kaci Smith, having been given prior knowledge—"

"I didn't think Dora meant it," he exclaimed. "I mean, people talk shit all the time, but they don't really mean it."

"—that there would be no blood on your hands?" the agent continued. "These girls would be alive." He leaned forward slightly. "You could have informed the police *anonymously.* Do you know what that word means?"

"Yeah, I know what it means. I'm not fucking stupid. I thought it was all bullshit. I swear to God, until I saw Ellyn, I thought it was all bullshit. I thought they'd totally fucking lied about Kaci. Just heard she was dead and, you know—"

"Made the claim?"

"Yeah! I mean, I *knew* Dust was lying. He's got this *thing.* His face twitches when he lies."

"But they weren't lying, were they? And what about after Ellyn was killed? Why not say something then?"

"They were going to say I'd done it! Don't you get it? They were going to blame the whole fucking thing on me?"

In the silence that followed that statement, I realized they were going to start talking about Madison next. "I'll be outside," I whispered to Graylin. She let go of me and I left. I needed air and space. I would definitely not be joining the ranks of the SBI. I was *so* not cut out for the life. I went to the water cooler and drank a cupful.

"Not so glamorous as one might think," a female voice said. "Huh?"

I looked over to see Laura sitting cross-legged on the floor against the wall. We were the only two people present in the room. "No," I replied. "Not glamorous."

"It makes me sick," she said. "The thought that went into it. The meticulous planning. The doer always think they're so superior, so much smarter than everyone else."

I walked over and slid down the wall next to her. Cool, solid floor had never felt so good. "Sometimes you hear about a murder in the news," I said, "—and you wonder what drives a person to kill like that. And then, in the end, it's nothing but stupid jealously?"

"It's a lot more than that," she said quietly. "Too often it's a lifetime of abuse and who know what else. But you know what? I'm not even sure it matters. I used to think so. I used to think it was really important to figure out what made serials tick. But, at the end of the day, Dora Blake is nothing but a twisted sociopath. Not only dangerous; she's toxic. The kind of person who makes you believe in the concept of capital punishment. This from someone who joined the bureau as a staunch opponent of the death penalty."

"You ever worry about how much the job will change you?"

She nodded. And then shook her head. "I'm not going to do it anymore." She sighed. "I'm done."

That was why she'd led me in instead of one of the others. "Where's Randy?"

"He's in one of the rooms. So are reps from the FBI, ATF and DEA. There are four interrogations going on right now, plus they're still at the Pegram house. This thing has gotten massive."

"Does he know I'm here?"

She shook her head.

"I should probably go," I said. "Wait outside for Graylin. But can I ask you one thing?"

She nodded. "What?"

"How did you guys know about Charlie? Her name, I mean."

"Ah. There have been a couple of clues left along the way," Laura replied hesitantly. "Not after the first one, but after the second. Ellyn. In the bathroom at the mall. There was a note on the mirror written in lipstick."

"Probably Kaci Smith's lipstick," I said, creeped out by the thought even as I put it into words.

"Yeah, it was."

"What did it say?"

"You want to see?"

I only hesitated a second before I nodded. "Yeah."

"Come on," she said getting up.

I used the wall to get up, although I tried not to make it obvious. I followed Laura to one of the bulletin boards, but rather than turn it around, we went behind it to look. And there was Ellyn's case on raw, unflinching display. I saw photographs of her dead body in my peripheral vision, but I didn't look directly at them. Instead, I honed in on the photograph of the mirror with its cryptic lipstick message and leaned closer to read. In vibrant pink, it said '*I'm not MAD but the next one will be.*'

"Oh, my God," I breathed.

"Yeah. Unfortunately, the meaning only became clear after Madison was discovered."

I was reeling from the fact that Dora had planned Madison's murder so much in advance. It was beyond sick. It was evil and twisted and … I couldn't come up with a bad enough word. "And Charlie?"

"A note arrived later. Written in blood."

I felt a cold shiver run up my spine and my mouth curled in disgust. "Madison's blood?"

She nodded. "You beginning to see it? How she was enjoying herself? Making a game out of it?"

Laura moved to the next board and I followed, although my legs felt wooden. *Madison's board.* I tried only to look at the photograph of the note because, somehow, Madison had become personal. I didn't want to see her wounds or her autopsy photos. The note read, '*I don't just kill young women. My next will be CHARLIE*'. I pressed a hand to the back of my neck and squeezed.

"We were thinking it would be a guy," Laura said. "We pulled reports of every male student in middle and high school named Charles."

"Charlie is only a kid," I said in a thick voice. "She's just this sweet, innocent girl. Plays soccer and doesn't want her brother to call her Charlotte."

"I know," she said.

"When did you know it was Dora?"

"We've looked at her from the second kill on, but we've got a dozen suspects, too. Female serial killers are an anomaly."

An anomaly, I thought. *Like a time warp.* I really needed some air. I decided I would go call Mom, but when we emerged from behind the bulletin board, I saw Graylin approaching.

"Ready?" Graylin asked me. "I'll drive you home."

I looked at Laura. "Thanks."

She nodded, and then Graylin and I left. The instant we stepped outside, the air and the darkness were a relief. We didn't speak most of the way home. I had tried not to look at the crime scene photos, but they must have registered in my peripheral vision because they were in my mind now, flashing their horror. "You didn't hear anything back there that shocked you, did you?" I finally asked, breaking the silence.

"No."

"No one ever said anything about the cuts on the foot."

"We always hold some things back."

I looked out the window.

"We didn't understand the significance of the mark on the foot at first. The E was written in cursive, sort of, but we didn't know if it was an E or an M or if it symbolized something else. And then the next was a three. Or so we thought."

"You think they'll catch her?"

"Oh, yeah. For sure." When we pulled to a stop in front of the apartment, she looked at me. "You okay?"

It took a moment to respond. "I didn't realize I had a weak stomach."

Her eyes suddenly blazed with unshed tears. "If you didn't feel sick to your stomach by what you just heard and saw, I wouldn't want a damn thing to do with you."

I was grateful for the sentiment.

"Call me if you need to talk," she said.

I nodded. "Thanks."

"You were a really important part of it."

"I'm glad. It was dumb luck, but I'm glad." I reached for the door handle. "Night."

"Goodnight."

I hesitated. "Will you be at school on Monday?"

"I don't know. Dora won't be dumb enough to show back up at school, but I'll be there if they tell me to be there."

~~~

On Sundays, the store is open from one until five and it's usually dead. That Sunday was no exception, for which I was thankful. I worked alone, also as usual, and I was glad for that, too. The events of the last few days had taken a toll. I kept trying to clear the things I'd heard and seen from my mind, but images or memories flared unexpectedly.

I'd just finished closing out the register when the bell mounted on the front door jingled. I'd had a total of three customers over the course of the entire day, none for the last two hours, but then five minutes before five, one walks in? I wanted to moan. But I looked over with a pleasant enough expression and saw it was Ty. "Hey."

He halted and held up his hands like a surgeon waiting for gloves. "Mother Matt, I come for absolution."

"I don't know, man, you may be a lost cause."

He continued to the front counter. "What's up?"

"Not much. Getting ready to close."

"Duh. Thus your limo service."

"Absolution is that important to you?"

"*Abb*solutely. No, seriously, I wanted to tell you that Mom's fixing this blow out breakfast tomorrow. It's a tradition. And you are cordially invited to join. I actually just assumed you were coming and then Nik reminded me that you probably didn't know about it."

"That sounds great."

"It's for strength. Getting through mid-terms and all." He pulled a cheesy looking racecar keychain off a display case and fiddled with the wheels. "So, you got time to hear a confession?"

"Why not? Just make it entertaining."

"I, ah … I'm not supposed to talk about it."

I could feel the shift. He wasn't joking anymore.

"Remember when you asked me if I was worried about Charlie? With all the shit's that's been going on?"

I nodded.

"This son of a bitch tried to grab her yesterday at school."

For a second, I didn't know how to respond. Obviously, I couldn't act like I knew, but it felt dishonest to act totally shocked. "Is she okay?"

He shrugged. "It scared her."

"I bet."

"It's so weird. These FBI guys were right there and on it. Man, they must be everywhere after all that's happened."

"I guess so."

"Course, now I have to spend the rest of my life worrying about her." He shook his head. "This shit needs to be over. Anyway, you can't tell anybody. It's being kept all hush-hush."

"I understand."

"I only told Nikki. And now you."

I felt honored by his trust. "I won't tell anyone."

"I know." He put the key chain back up and headed for the door. "Vows of secrecy and all that. So, you ready? Let's blow this pop-cycle stand."

I grabbed my keys and headed to the door where I turned out lights.

When Ty stopped in front of our apartment building, he said, "Seven thirty. I'll be right here."

"You don't need to. I'll walk over."

He gave me a look. "Are you always going to be this big a pain in the ass?"

I laughed, got out of the car and he drove off.

I was in a good mood until I walked in the apartment and saw mom stretched out on the couch, watching TV. We'd barely spoken or even seen each other since the night I met Dave and she I had words. She saw me, muted the TV and waved me over.

I didn't budge. "What?"

She sat up. "This isn't going to be what you want to hear."

"Then don't say it."

"Hey, you know what? I can say if I want to. And I'm going to. I love the guy."

I couldn't speak for a second. She's said a lot of things about her men over the years, but never that. "Yeah, well what about me?" I asked, knowing I sounded petulant.

"What about you? Look, this is my chance. And I swear to God it's the last time."

"When have I heard that before?"

"Don't be an asshole," she replied, frowning with irritation.

"So, that's it?"

"I'm not doing this to hurt you, you know."

"But I don't think you really care that it hurts me, either."

She drew breath to speak but didn't for several seconds. "This is my chance, Matty. It's my shot at being happy."

There was nothing else to say, so I turned and went to my room. I sat on the bed, suddenly too tired to move. Finally, I called Graylin, and got her voicemail. "Hey, it's me," I said when I got the beep. "I just learned we're moving to Charlotte. Once again, my life is torn the hell up. But so what? Worse things happen. Right?"

I only had to think of Ellyn and Madison and Kaci to be put in my place. So we'd move to Charlotte and I'd probably go back to being a recluse. So what? I'd been one most of my life before the past weeks had changed everything. I'd get through my senior year and then go on to college and the rest of my life, just as I'd always planned. Worse things had most definitely happened. "I'll talk to you later." I closed my phone and lay back on the bed, so depressed that the center of my chest ached.

16

The girl in the red shirt

I woke early and walked to the Larkin's the next morning. Their street, Forestdale Avenue, bustled with normal, morning activity, the kind you see in coffee commercials. Little kids goofing as they waited for the bus. Adults leaving for work with travel mugs and various objects in hand. American dream stuff.

Ty jogged out to his car just as I reached the house. "Hey, Larkin," I called.

He turned to me. "I was just coming to get you. Hurry up if you want to get any food."

My stomach rumbled at the scent of bacon. "I can smell it from here."

"So, Kenny Jameson called last night and guess who got in a big fight with some guys from Southwest?"

"Who?"

"Jay Fields, Nathan Mattocks, David Seymore and like five or six other guys. It got ugly and Fields had his shoulder dislocated."

Just the thought of a dislocated shoulder caused a twinge of pain.

"Coach is so pissed. So, I'm thinking this is the time. We send word that Triple M is coming and he need not worry. The season will be well in hand. I knew you were going to rock it next year, but why wait?"

I opened my mouth to break the news that I was moving to Charlotte, but then shut it again. I really didn't want to get into it at that moment. "Maybe."

"Not maybe. Definetely."

We walked into the kitchen through the carport, and I saw a glorious array of food set out everywhere. It smelled amazing.

Kids were filling plates and chatting up a storm and more sat around the table.

"Hi, Matt," Tina Larkin said with a warm smile.

"Hi, Mrs. Larkin."

"You know Eric Evans?" Ty asked me.

I started to shake my head, but Eric spoke first. "We were in Latin last semester," he said.

I nodded like I remembered him. "That's right."

"And this is Amanda," Nikki spoke up. "We've been best friends since the third grade. Isn't that crazy?"

"It's great," I said. And I meant it. I can only imagine knowing the same people for most of your life.

"Let's eat," Ty said.

Everyone else had either helped themselves or were filling plates. There were pancakes and scrambled eggs and bacon and cut up fruit and fat blueberry muffins.

"Can we do this every Monday, Mrs. Larkin?" Mike asked.

"No way," she declared. "It's exhausting!"

I tried to shake the thought that this was all going away. I was moving to Charlotte just when I'd started to fit in. Some people were sitting at the kitchen table, but Steph and Morgan carried their plate into the other room. Steph gave me a look of invitation that arrived loud and clear. It was not one that I wanted to accept.

"There's orange juice and apple juice on the table," Tina said as she poured herself a cup of coffee.

"Or coffee," Ty added. "Or screwdrivers."

"Such a funny guy," his mother chided.

Ty sat at the table and started eating. "Killer pancakes, Mom," he said a second later, his mouth full.

I walked over and claimed one of the two empty spots left at the kitchen table and sat, feeling that conspicuous, out of place thing again. Nikki, seated next to me, asked, "What do you have today?"

"History and Chemistry," I said.

"What do you have?" Nikki asked Amanda.

Amanda's upper lip curled. "Psych and Algebra two."

136

"That sucks," Ty commiserated.

Charlie came into the kitchen, looking shy.

"Hey, Charlotte," Ty said. "You want some pancakes before I eat them all?"

"If you eat them all, *Tyrone*, Mom'll just make me more."

"I don't think so. She's out of the stuff."

Charlie looked at her mom and Tina gave her a cockeyed smile and shook her head.

"I think he's just messing with you, Charlie," I offered.

Charlie grinned, blushed and nodded, as if we were sharing a confidence.

"Don't be flirting with my friends, Charlotte," Ty said.

"You want me to kick him for you?" Nikki asked Charlie in an exasperated voice.

Charlie nodded.

"Ouch," Ty yelled, even though Nikki was sitting too far away to reach him.

"That's what you get," Nikki teased. "Leave her alone."

"You want some pancakes, sweetheart?" Tina said. "Or a muffin?"

Charlie shrugged one shoulder. She looked so shy and out of place that I felt for her, although I felt pretty much the same. "Want me to save this seat for you?" I asked, patting the empty chair next to me.

She nodded but didn't look at me.

"Well, then hurry or somebody else will try to get it and then I'll have to fight them," I said.

Grinning, she turned and went to the kitchen island to grab a plate. I glanced at Tina and she smiled at me.

"This is so good, Tina," Nikki said. "Thank you."

A whole chorus of thank-you rang out. Ty added a 'ma'am' for good measure.

"You're welcome," Tina laughed. "Everyone has to go ace their tests, now."

"I don't know about acing," Amanda said, "But here's to passing."

"I'll drink to that," Ty said.

All our glasses went into the air.

"Especially biology," Ty said.

"Especially Spanish," Eric added.

Steph came in from the other room with her plate and glass in hand and, unfortunately, slid into the seat next to me. I looked over and saw Charlie freeze. She was midway to the table, plate in hand. I waved her over and scooted over on my chair. Then Nikki scooted over to share her chair with me. Charlie came forward hesitantly and sat next to me.

"Oh, I'm sorry," Steph said, halfway getting back up. "Did I take your place?"

Charlie shook her head, embarrassed.

"That's okay," I said. "We like to share."

Charlie kept her face down but smiled and blushed again. She blushed easily and every single time she did I felt my heart squeeze a little.

"That way," I said, "if she gets something that looks good, I can just reach over and take it."

Charlie knocked into me, playfully.

"Hey," I complained. "I didn't even try to grab anything yet. I was going to wait until you were looking the other way."

"You have any tests today, Charlie?" Steph asked.

I felt Nikki stiffen.

Charlie shook her head.

"Lucky," Steph said.

"Has anyone had Pitchford for Spanish?" Eric asked.

I felt Nikki relax at the change of subjects.

"I did," Amanda said.

"How was the mid-term?"

"Tough," Amanda admitted. "But Spanish wasn't my thing."

Charlie started eating. Tina walked over with a glass of orange juice, and I took it and set it down for her.

"You're such a natural," Nikki said to me.

"Hey, Matthews," Ty said. "Don't be flirting with my girl. Either of them."

I looked at Charlie and rolled my eyes, and she giggled.

138

After breakfast, we loaded up in cars and drove to school. I felt terrific and strangely free. Breakfast had been fun, and the worst of everything was behind us. Charlie was skittish, but she would be okay. The bad guys had mostly been caught and there was little doubt that, in time, Dora would be, too. Mid-terms didn't worry me. At the moment, even the thought of moving to Charlotte didn't worry me. I'd deal with it when I had to.

We parked and made our way toward the main entrance *en masse*, a new experience for me. I was approaching the front doors when my phone vibrated. I retrieved it from my backpack and saw it was Graylin calling. "Hey," I answered, dodging incomers as I segued to the side of the building. "Good timing. I was like a second away from walking in the door."

"I need you to think," she said in a grim tone.

I felt a weird, warning tingle up the back of my neck. "Okay. Sure. What's going on?"

"Think back on every time you ever saw Dora and her group." She paused. "It was always that group of three guys hanging around her, right?"

"Yeah. Why?"

"Do you remember ever seeing anyone else with them?"

"Um, no, but I'd never even noticed them before everything happened."

"Yeah, you definitely aren't the world's most observant."

"Why are you asking?"

"Because of an email we got last night."

"An email?"

"Yeah, an email claiming that Dora wasn't responsible for the murders. That she's a wannabe. That her claim is all about getting attention."

"Maybe she wrote it herself. To cast doubt."

"Unfortunately, it's signed from a name we've seen before. A name we never made public." She paused. "A name associated with other murders. Unsolved murders."

Whoa. "Maybe the emailer is trying to claim credit for something they didn't do," I suggested lamely. "I mean, there's no doubt about what Dora did. Right? What about Luke's confession?"

"We've been over it and over it. No one who's talking actually witnessed her killing anyone."

"Can you trace the guy through his email?"

"No. The son of a bitch knows how to play."

"How can she be a wannabe when she picked out the victims?"

"It's possible she was *used* by mystery guy. That doesn't make her any less guilty, but think of her as a puppet, and he's the puppet master playing all of us. He let Dora pick the victims. That's how it worked in Fayetteville a couple of years ago." The bell rang. "I heard that. You better go, but if you think of anybody—"

"Yeah. I'll let you know."

"Hey, about moving to Charlotte, is that a definite?"

"Given it's my mom?" I asked wryly. "Who knows? I hope not."

"I hope not, too. Bye."

I got through my mid-terms despite the nonstop racking of my brain for every time I'd ever seen Dora Blake, and every person I'd ever seen her with. But I had never noticed her until that fateful rainy morning Mom drove me to school. I wasn't going to stumble upon the magic answer this time. I sat in English doodling because I'd already finished (actually rereading) The Count of Monte Cristo which everyone else was still slogging through.

As I sat there, trying to sketch Sirena, I decided I was going to be to be open to new people and experiences next year. I'd go for soccer or track or both. If it didn't work out, so what? I'd survived rejection before. It bruised, but it didn't kill. It embarrassed, but it didn't annihilate. Okay, it had annihilated me in middle school, but I wasn't a kid anymore.

I glanced at the clock on the wall and saw it was 3:03. The girl sitting next to me snuck a yellow and green gummy worm, and then offered me one. I was about to accept when my eye caught on movement in the hall. Dora had just strutted past the open door of the classroom. Shock reverberated through my entire body like jabs of electricity.

"What's wrong?" the girl whispered.

I stood. I didn't want to believe what I'd just seen – but I'd just seen it. With my heart hammering and my mind racing, I moved toward the door.

"Matt?" Mr. Smith, my English teacher said. "Something you need?"

Dora was there! I poked my head out the door a split second before she turned at the next hall. On her back was a backpack and at her side was a gun. *Could she have just waltzed in here with a gun?* I turned back to see every eye in the room upon me. I swallowed hard, fumbled for my cell and began texting Graylin, but I was so nervous, I kept misspelling the words.

"Matt? What in the world?" Mr. Smith exclaimed.

Like in most schools, cell phones are banned at North. Not that we don't all have them and spend about half the day texting when the teachers aren't looking.

"Everyone should get against this inside wall, and you should lock the door," I said. I reached over and turned out the lights. I'd managed to send **Dora here with gun I tink.** Close enough. It was what I tought. Mr. Smith's jaw had gone lax. "Call the office and tell them someone may have a weapon." I heard several sharp gasps as I stepped into the hall and followed that path Dora had taken.

"Matt!" Mr. Smith called.

I heard the concern in his voice. After all, I'd never done one attention grabbing thing, and AP English was a year-long class. I hadn't even made it to the next hall when the gut-wrenching chatter of an automatic weapon halted me in my tracks. I'd only heard it on movies and games but I knew exactly what it was. The shiver that traveled down my spine was painful. Unless I missed my guess, Dora knew she was caught, so she just wanted to kill as many people as possible.

I forced myself into motion again. As I passed the next room, I looked over and saw a girl freeze as she reached to shut the door. She was thin, her eyes were wide and frightened, and her shirt was red. It was my recurrent dream happening in real life. My stomach was so tight, I felt sick. I pressed on it, and kept moving forward, but it was like gravity had thickened around me. It was hard to move.

Faces kept flashing in my mind's eye.

My mom.

Sirena.

Graylin.

Ty.

Nikki.

Charlie

Mrs. Lane, my fourth-grade teacher.

I pictured people it didn't even make sense to think about. Suzanne Farlow, Steph and these giggling girls waiting for the elementary school bus I'd seen that morning.

I heard the sound of crying ahead and knew the room Dora was in. Part of me wanted to turn and bolt, but how could I when I'd been clued into all this? Maybe it was my fate. How had I dreamt about the girl in the red shirt if it wasn't? I moved closer to the door, took a couple of deep breaths and peeked in to see where she was.

The back of the room had been vacated. No kids sat there, although their books and shit were still there. Dora was sitting on a desk facing the front of the room where the teacher and all the students stood scared out of their minds. Most of them were crying. She held one gun, an automatic handgun, and a longer gun was next to her on the desk. There was a hole blown in the ceiling. I backed away and leaned against the edge of the locker, struggling to breathe and trying to decide whether to text Graylin again to pass on Dora's location.

"Never a female," Dora was saying. "Which is insane when you consider we have the sharper minds. I mean, guys can be made to do anything. You wouldn't believe what I've made guys do."

"Pardon the interruption," the principal boomed over the loudspeaker, making me jump. "Will Mr. Marshal come to the front office? Marshal to the office. This is not a drill."

Dora laughed. "Did you hear that? This is not a drill. Holy fucking God! Give the genius a medal."

Down the hall, classroom lights were turning off and doors were being shut and locked.

"Who wants to die first?" Dora asked conversationally. "You?"

A girl broke into hysterics.

Shit. I had to get in there and try to get the guns away from her. If I could sneak in from behind without her noticing, there was a chance. I'd just have to grab her and the gun long enough for everyone else to move in and help subdue her. Seconds. We were only talking seconds.

"You?" Dora asked.

"No, please," a guy cried.

"Miss Blake," a man said, obviously the teacher. "Please!"

"Please what? Maybe it should be you."

A girl lost it and began crying hysterically which was the distraction I needed. I don't think I was breathing at all as I went in. I was trying to move fast and silently, but kids in the front of the classroom looked at me, alarming Dora who whirled around to me.

I jerked to a stop and raised my hands so that she wouldn't shoot, but there was an explosion of noise and pain, and then I was on my back, staring at the ceiling, unable to breathe. I was vaguely aware that there was chaos, movement, screaming and distant gunfire from another part of the building. Which meant there were more shooters there. Which meant the carnage I'd seen in my trance was going to happen. I'd thought it had been prevented when the makings of bombs had been found, but I was wrong.

I pictured Sirena, and then blackness pressed in, suffocating me.

17

RU 2

The blackness began lightening.

I was alive?

I was alive! I was disoriented, but I was standing. And I was naked. I felt rough surface on one side of me and I was aware of a woman on my other side. I tried to focus, but I was confused by the place and the fact it was night. There were bright searchlights darting here and there. I knew something was happening. Something bad. There were sounds of distress and a feeling of palpable tension. I noticed red lines from a laser light forming in the distance.

"Is he all right?" I heard a guy ask.

"I don't know." (That had been Sirena's voice.) "Matt?"

She touched me and my vision cleared. Sirena stood to my side and one of the twins was next to her. We were probably fifty yards away from where frightened people were being herded into large, square conveyances made of something that looked like yellow-tinted Plexiglas.

"Here," the twin said. He shrugged off his tunic and handed it over.

I quickly put it on. At least it covered the essentials. "Thanks."

"Are you stable?" Sirena asked urgently, squeezing my arm.

I nodded, not fully trusting the fact that I was all right. But I seemed to be whole and unhurt. Of course, that was here and now.

Here? Now?

Hadn't I just been shot? I'd wanted to help, to get the gun from Dora, but had I done any good at all, or had I made a bad situation worse?

"Shit," the twin muttered. "They're widening the grid."

The laser-like lines of red light were beginning to expand in choppy, foot-wide increments.

Sirena's hand tightened on my arm. "Let's go," she urged, backing up.

I followed, but immediately tripped on something, Only hers and the twin's hands stopped me from a face plant. Panicked by the few second delay, we ran full out. I glanced behind us to see the grid snaking toward us with a seeming vengeance. We ducked into a narrow alley just ahead of a beam that rocketed by us.

"Run like you have never run," the twin cried.

I did and I'm a strong runner, but they were as fast or even faster. A line of pulsating light pursued us. It seemed alive and determined – but it couldn't be. It was only light. Right? "What is it?" I called.

"It's the fuckin' DC grid," the twin called back. "Do not let it touch you!"

Sirena started up a fire escape as fast as her arms and legs would go. It was dangerously rickety and noisy as we ascended. I experienced an irrational fear about the light hearing us but mostly I concentrated on keeping pace. I was between Sirena and the twin, who was probably in last place to protect me. I didn't know what a DC grid meant, but it was clearly a threat. I reached the landing of the third floor and saw the lines beginning to rise in a sizzling, translucent curtain. "It's coming!"

Sirena tried the fire door to the third floor, just as she'd tried the one below, but it was locked. We headed up another flight to the fourth floor, all of us badly winded. That door was locked, too.

"We won't make it to the roof in time," the twin declared.

He looked around in a panic and I did the same. There was a slightly open window several feet away from the fire escape. Getting to it would not be the easiest thing, but it wasn't impossible either. We were only a minute or so from being caught in the grid, so there was no time to think. I gripped the rusty banister of the fire escape and jumped over it and onto the narrow window ledge, cutting my hand in the process. My knee hit the glass, but it didn't break. The impact threw me wildly off balance and, for a terrifying second, I tipped backwards.

The twin, reaching way over the rail, braced me or I would have fallen. I regained enough balance to grip the base of the window. I tried to pull it up, but it wouldn't budge. I felt a cold sweat break out all over me. It suddenly gave way, and I scrambled through and opened it wider. The others followed, but red light filled the window. We jumped away from it, not knowing if we were caught or not. At least, I didn't know.

We flattened ourselves against the inside wall and frantically crept sideways, keeping just beyond the perimeter of the red glare. The whole room pulsed with an angry energy, but we shoved ourselves into a shadowed corner until it withdrew.

"We need out of here," Sirena said in a shaky voice. "Now!"

"Two of you still?" a deep voice said. *Aidan.*

"Three," the twin said.

"Hold tight," the deep voice answered. "Bringing you in."

"What was that?" I asked quietly.

"A detection and containment grid," Sirena replied. "If it touches you, you're caught."

"And it fuckin' hurts," the twin said.

"Your presence is registered, and they come after you," Sirena said.

"They usually keep the grid smaller," the twin added. "It doesn't spread like that. Did you get the feeling they were after us?"

I felt Sirena quiver. "Yes.

I gasped because of a deadening, tingling feeling all over. And then we were back in the room I'd first seen Aiden and Dairy and Smoke and the others. This time, only about a half dozen people were there, including Dairy and Ji. They all looked exhausted and frazzled. Some had small, electronic devices with screens in hand, but I couldn't make out what was on the screens. It was changing too rapidly.

"You hurt?" Dairy asked, her violet gaze sweeping over all of us.

"No," the twin replied. "But that was one determined grid search. Almost like they were expecting us."

"They're looking to exterminate all of us in one night," Dairy seethed. "And they just may do it. The fuckers!"

"Hello, Matt," Ji said with a look of intense suspicion. "Interesting timing on your part. Where did you come from?"

"I brought him over," Sirena declared angrily. "You have a problem with that?"

"Interesting timing was all I said," Ji said.

"Good thing he was there," the twin added. "Or we probably wouldn't be."

"What happened?" Dairy demanded.

"The grid was spreading," the twin began. "We barely made it to this old building and sprinted up a fire escape that was so dilapidated, I thought we might send the whole thing flying. Floor two, the door is locked. Same on three and four. Meanwhile, the fuckin' light's moving faster than we can. We spotted a barely open window maybe three feet away, and Matt jumps. Almost loses his shit, but he recovered and made it through. We all id, but barely."

"Impressive," Ji said. Only he didn't seem impressed. He seemed convinced that I was an operative of the Foundation. "First you show up out of nowhere and then you rescue two of our best."

Sirena sent Ji a withering look. "Hey, Ji?"

His look was deadpan as he shifted his gaze to her. "Yeah?"

"Fuck you. You insult him, you insult me."

"Your hand," Dairy said to me.

I looked down and saw the blood. I hadn't realized how badly I'd sliced it open.

Dairy went to an open bag, rifled through it and came up with a pair of pants, a bottle and a cloth and came to me with the pants slung over her shoulder. She inspected my hand and then began tending to it, first pouring the solution over it, which didn't hurt at all, and then wiping gently. The bleeding stopped at once.

"That doesn't even sting," I commented.

"It will," she said dispassionately. "Like a mother fucker."

And then it did. My eyes bulged and I started to double over. It felt like my hand had been dunked in acid.

"Put on some pants," Dairy said as she handed them over.

I took a shaky few steps away and put them on. Gratefully. It's hard to feel dignity when you're pantlesss.

"I've got Ocean," a woman exclaimed while staring at her screen.

The announcement caused excitement.

"Where?" Ji asked.

"Southeast. RU 9."

Ji studied his own device and sighed with relief as he, too, saw it. He nodded at Dairy. "It's Ocean, Glass and it looks like three more. They're safe."

"What's happened since we left?" the twin asked urgently.

The pain in my hand had passed, leaving it cold and numb. It was also shiny, the cut coated and sealed.

"Libs is trying to connect with Smoke now," Dairy replied.

"Who?" Sirena asked

"The new girl. Lexy. The blonde?"

"The one who looks fourteen?" the twin asked, looking disturbed. "Is she up to it?"

"She's eighteen," Dairy snapped. "Not as young as Seery was when she joined us. Is she up to it? We don't know, but we're running short of candidates, in case you haven't noticed."

"Oh, really," the twin replied with mock seriousness. "Thanks for pointing that out, Dairy."

Sirena looked at me. "There was a raid. Teddy was tagged and taken to DeCory," she explained quietly. "Smoke went in after him."

"We got Teddy back," Dairy said, shaking her head. "But—"

"But?" the twin repeated.

"It's not good," Dairy stated grimly. She went back to the bag and dropped the bottle in. The rag she tossed to the floor.

"What's DeCory?" I asked Sirena.

She looked at me curiously. "The Detention Center. The maze."

I'd never heard of DeCory.

The twin stalked off and Sirena indicated we should follow.

"Thank you," I said to Dairy before I trailed after Sirena.

Dairy nodded, Ji still looked suspicious, and everyone else continued to monitor their trackers. The twin, Sirena and I made our way down a corridor and my mind raced with all I'd been told and everything I'd been through.

"Get us there, will you?" the twin said.

Sirena stepped closer to me. "Keep walking, but close your eyes," she said as she put one arm around me and the other on my chest, which made it hard to focus on anything else. I closed my eyes and experienced rushy movement. When it let up, I opened my eyes to find that we were somewhere else.

"Which twin are you?" I spoke up, wanting to focus on something other than my traitorously wobbly legs.

"You can't tell?"

There was too much tension in the air for it to be as amusing as it might have otherwise been.

"Gabe," Sirena supplied.

We approached one of the stone wall archways and Sirena stuck her hand out as if she were giving it some sort of salute. A small circle in the center of her hand suddenly glowed with a soft blue light and with a distinct *slp slp* sound, one I'd heard once before. The wall slid open. We stepped through and it shut behind us.

"You have some sort of control mechanism imbedded in your hand?" I asked.

"We have lots of secret compartments," Gabe replied. "We have to. This is war and we're the rebels. Remember?"

"This is the infirmary," Sirena said, jutting her chin forward. "Teddy will be here."

149

We went to a large window and looked into a sterile looking room and a patient lying on a cot. We could only see his feet since one of the gowned attendants blocked his upper body from view. The attendant moved, but Teddy was unrecognizable after a brutal beating.

The sight was nauseating.

Gabe pressed a fist to the window. "He's not going to make it, is he?" he said under his breath.

"And Smoke will have died for nothing," Sirena grieved.

I turned away because the sight of Teddy was making me feel dangerously sick to my stomach.

Gabe stepped back from the glass, shaking with rage. He turned around as if looking for something or someone to punch. "Mother fuckers! I want them dead! I want them all dead!" He moved to the stone wall, having reared back to punch it, but his motion slowed as his fist moved toward the surface.

It was Sirena. She was doing this, slowing his motion. Protecting him from himself. But it was causing a great strain on her.

Help me, she beckoned silently.

I had no idea how to, but I closed my eyes and willed her my strength. I experienced a drain of energy, and then Gabe called her name. He was leaning against the wall, his forehead pressed to it. I looked down at his hand and was relieved that it was intact. He hadn't broken or even bloodied it.

Sirena slumped to the floor in exhaustion, and I sat next to her, feeling as drained as she looked. Gabe turned and looked at us and then he, too, slid down the wall and sat with his legs splayed out.

"Men are idiots," Sirena said in a flat voice. She wiped tears from her face with both hands and sniffed.

"Yeah," Gabe agreed tiredly. "And even when we know we're being idiots, we can't seem to stop ourselves."

"Smoke went into the maze to get Teddy?" I asked, still not sure what had transpired.

Sirena nodded. "She let herself get swept up in a grid search."

"Then how is he here and she's not?"

She looked at me. "She killed him to save him. We don't know how she got to him to do that, but—"

I had no idea what she was talking about.

Gabe spoke up. "When they said Lexy was working to connect with Smoke? That's because Smoke is still there. Trapped in the maze. Good and trapped now that she sprung Teddy. See, to get out of the maze, you have to be released or you have to be dead. Because when you're dead, you have no body heat, and their containment field can't hold you."

My mind spun from the realization that Smoke had killed the man she loved in order to possibly save him, all the while, knowing the act would damn her. "How did she kill him?"

"We have a capsule of naira in one of our secret compartments." Gabe replied.

"What's naira?"

He leaned his head back against the wall. "A very effective poison."

In one of their secret compartments. Meaning implanted. Under their skin, within their bodies.

"It stops the heart within seconds," Sirena said. "But we have an antidote as long as we can get the body back within three or four minutes of ingestion."

"Did you find out anything about who made the game?" Gabe asked.

"His name is Cres Singledon."

Gabe's head jerked up. He looked so alarmed, Sirena and I both stared.

"You know the name?" Sirena asked Gabe.

He shook his head, but he seemed stricken. "No."

"Chris, you said?" Sirena asked, glancing at me.

"Cres. C-R-E-S."

Gabe didn't look like he was breathing.

"Gabe, what is it?" Sirena asked.

"What else did you learn?" Gabe pushed. "Anything? Did you see his picture?"

"I only found one. He appears to be really reclusive, so there aren't many. He's not quite thirty. Good looking. Brown hair, kind of wavy. He has—"

"What?" Sirena asked when my sentence was left hanging.

I'd been about to say he had this memorable smile when it occurred to me whose smile it reminded me of. Gabe and Westin. His smile was exactly like theirs, his faces quite similar to theirs. "This great smile," I finished.

"I gotta go," Gabe said, getting to his feet. He walked away with what looked like great purpose, raising his hand when he got to the doorway. The center of the back of his hand glowed with a dark green circle.

"What was that?" Sirena asked.

I didn't know what to say.

"Matt! Who is Cres Singledon?"

I looked at her resignedly. "Do Gabe and Westin have a brother?"

Her eyes widened and then she looked off in the direction Gabe had gone.

"Just a guess," I said quickly.

She looked back at me. "Yes, they have a brother. Daniel. He's brilliant. A scientist on Rowan-Bachna. He's responsible for a lot of our technology. But it couldn't be him. You have to be wrong."

I nodded, ready to agree with her.

"Although," she murmured. "If there is anyone capable of manipulating a wormhole, it would be him." She worried her bottom lip, hating the suspicion.

The wall slid open again and Dairy walked toward us like a determined Amazon warrior. "Libs is coming out of it. We may need you," she said to Sirena.

"Coming," Sirena said.

Dairy left.

Sirena got to her feet and offered me a hand. "Don't say anything while we're in there," she said quietly when we stood face to face. "I'll explain everything later."

I nodded.

We followed Dairy into an opening that led to a domed, oval room, although my step slowed because the sight was so strange. The curved wall was made of something clear but foggy looking. The floor was the opaque glass I'd seen in corridors, and light emanated through it which gave the three people standing ominous looking shadows to their faces. Dairy, Aiden, and a guy I didn't know. A blonde girl was stretched on a recliner wrapped up in something. She looked deeply asleep.

The door *slp* shut behind us and I stopped and glanced around. Aiden was tense. It was apparent he had way too much adrenalin flowing and no outlet for it. A tall guy with a sharp nose, hovered over the girl on the stretcher thing. She really did look fourteen.

"Lexy?" sharp nose said. "We need you to come back now."

For a moment, there was no response, and then she moaned softly and twitched.

"Good," sharp nose soothed. "Follow my voice."

The chair was moving, slowly sitting her up and gently gyrating, as if to wake her. *Whoa.* I definitely wanted to try it. Some of the arms of the device, which had enfolded her, withdrew. Now it reminded me of some primordial creature releasing its offspring.

Or its prey.

"Come on, Little Bit," Aiden called impatiently.

Dairy moved closer to Libs, leaned over her and patted her cheek lightly. "Wake up, Lexy."

Lexy's eyes fluttered and she moaned again.

"Get the stuff," Dairy said to Sirena. "I think she went in pretty deep."

Sirena went to a table and poured something from a bottle into a small cup and brought it to Dairy.

"Come on, babe, drink this," Dairy said, motioning to the chair to heft Lexy higher, which it did. She brought the cup to the girl's lips. "It does the trick."

Lexy managed a drink and then practically gagged. She moaned, shook her head and pushed it away.

"What are you saying?" Dairy teased. "You don't want to have it with dinner?"

"Did you get her?" Aiden demanded as he came closer.

"Give her a fuckin' minute, will you?" Dairy snapped at him.

"There is no fuckin' time! We need a stronger mind link on this and Sirena's here now."

"I got her," Libs assured them weakly.

Everyone looked at her. She nodded. "She wants to know about Teddy." Her words were slurred.

"She begin ripping?" Aiden asked.

Libs shook her head slowly. "She wants to know about Teddy first."

Dairy smirked at Aiden. "That's our girl."

"Yeah, well, we got protocol," Aiden thundered. "As she fucking well knows."

"Don't be a bitch," Dairy thundered back. "This is Smoke we're talking about and she had to kill Teddy. Remember? What if you had to end me?"

"You might not want to ask that right this minute," he retorted.

Ah ha.

Dairy looked at Libs. "Let her know that Teddy's here," she said. "He's fighting to make it."

Libs nodded.

Aiden moved to the base of the chair that now reminded me of a bear rug. "Get her to rip. We need to know her location."

"I know," Lexy whispered.

"Libs," the guy with the sharp nose spoke up from opposite Dairy. "Do you think you could speak aloud when you're connected?"

Dairy looked pained. "She hasn't had the training, Dom."

It looked Dom, Aiden and Dairy had Lexy pinned on three sides. I edged a little closer.

Dom smiled tenderly at Lexy who was watching him. "You are a natural if I've ever seen one."

She gave him a weak smile in return.

"We'll put trodes in place that help stimulate your ability," Dom continued. "You just have to—"

"Dom," Aiden snapped. "We got no time."

"—stay loose and let yourself go," Dom finished as if he hadn't spoken. "Your focus has to be on Smoke, but also on passing on what she says."

"I've seen it done," she said. "I could try projection, too."

Dom shrugged. "Projection is tough, but yeah. It can't hurt to try. Smoke is strong and experienced, so she'll be a great subject to mirror. She'll help on her end." He stepped back and busied himself placing electrodes in place on Libs' forehead and temples with quick precision.

Aiden exhibited his impatience with a loud sigh and Dairy gave him a black look and a jerk of her head.

He shook his head, a pawing bull ready to charge, and withdrew to the farthest point he could. His struggle to contain his barely caged fury filled the room.

"Connect as completely as you can," Dom coaxed. "You'll become a screen. Smoke's on one side of it and we're on the other."

Libs nodded and closed her eyes. The chair began reclining and growing fuller, so much so that Libs sunk into it. A soft airy sound filled the room. We all watched Libs, but nothing happened. I looked at Dom, whose full concentration was on Lexy. He was a good guy. A healer. Way intelligent and underestimated.

Sirena looked as if she was barely breathing. She was vulnerable and yet so strong. Had she been orphaned? What had made her the way she was? I wanted to know everything. I loved her. Full out, no holds barred loved her.

And what about Dairy's softer side? Was there one? Everything about her seemed to have a finely honed edge. She was someone you would want on your side. Fiercely loyal. Not that they all weren't but she would strike to kill anyone or anything who threatened one of hers. Of that I had no doubt.

Aiden wasn't all bluster, but he really did have all of this strength and passion and it had to go somewhere.

Lexy muttered something, drawing my attention back to her.

Dairy looked at Dom and shook her head.

Dom inclined his head and raised a hand as if begging for patience.

"Heh," Libs murmured. "Fii ta make it."

Her words were slow and slurred, but understandable.

"Rip," Aiden said.

Dom shook his head at Aiden.

"Rip," Libs whispered.

Sirena had silently worked her way next to me. Now she whispered in my ear, "Relevant information and personal requests."

"Female, twenty-eight," Libs said, speaking slowly. "I go by Smoke. My passname is … la … Laurel Kennedy. I'm tier five, one of five."

Dairy was nodding.

"I'm DEC. We're stationed at RU Two." A long paused ensued. "Tired," she muttered.

"Is that Libs or Smoke saying that?" Dairy asked Dom quietly.

Dom didn't reply because of the fuzzy, three-dimensional picture appearing around us. The curved wall and ceiling were filled with a sharpening image. A line of people. Waiting. Frightened. At the front of the line stood an officer and a leathery looking humanoid with a misshapen head and reptilian yellow eyes.

"They use psychic readers," Libs said, speaking as if it was difficult to get the words out. "Separate anyone with knowledge of rebel intelligence. I was tagged."

The picture on the screen changed. Now, a man with a badly scarred face was leaning close with a syringe in hand. At some point in time, one side of his face had been lacerated deeply and not sewn back together correctly.

"Tell us what you know," he threatened. And it was actually *his* voice coming from the screen, which took my breath. He squirted a small amount of black liquid from the

syringe. "Or we go again, and it will hurt more than the last."
He lifted a brow. "No?" He shrugged slightly and loomed
closer. Libs screamed in pain.

I jumped.

Sirena took hold of my hand. The picture had vanished.
Then an older, heavyset man with pockmarked skin came into
focus, Letters. He was Letters from the game. I looked over at
Sirena, who looked right back at me and then jerked her
attention back to study his face.

"Courage is an excellent quality," Letters said in a British-
accented voice. "But be warned, my dear. No one withstands
the sort of … shall we say, persuasion that we're so very good
at. There will be a breaking point. There always is. Why not
save yourself the pain and indignity?"

"Why not … fuck yourself?" Smoke retorted.

Scarface, standing to the side of letters, rolled up his
sleeves. "I like to start with my hands," he said as he held his
hands out and flexed them. "I like the ache in them at the end of
the day. Means it's been a good day." He reared back and
backhanded Smoke. We didn't see it, but we heard the impact
followed by a soft cry from Libs.

The viewpoint went sideways, and I nearly reeled with it.
Smoke, in her defiance, must have looked at him again, because
there he was. Letters looked on, utterly impassive. Rearing back
again, Scarface began slapping and then punching.

Sirena had drawn her fists to her face, as if she could hide
behind them. Dairy looked murderous. Only Dom looked
expressionless as he hovered over Libs. I got the feeling he was
aiding her somehow. Lending her strength, the way I'd just
done with Sirena to protect Gabe.

"You don't have to do this, you know," Letters spoke up.
"Tell us what you know, and we'll reconsider this interview."

"I know … you should lose weight," Libs slurred slowly,
speaking as Smoke.

Scarface loomed, and the screen went black.

"She's protecting us," Dairy said.

Aiden walked up behind her and pulled her back against him. Her arms crossed over his. "Is it done?" he asked Dom.

Dom shook his head and shrugged. "I don't know," he whispered.

An image appeared. Cutter. Handsome, infamous Cutter. "You've had your chance," he said to Letters. "Now release her to me."

Letters huffed. "What do you think you can manage that we can't?"

"Did I make it sound like a request?" Cutter asked coldly.

Letters looked insulted. "For how long?" he bit out.

Cutter looked at him as if he were a slimy bug on the floor. "For as long as I choose," he replied arrogantly.

Letters turned an enraged reddish purple. "Just because you're the Foundation's golden boy—"

"Take it up with them," Cutter said. He looked at Smoke with an unfathomable expression. "You took a beautiful, useful woman and reduce her to this. For what?"

Letters stalked from the room.

Cutter flicked his eyes to Scarface. "Get out."

Scarface made a slower, more relaxed exit.

Cutter produced a knife and leaned toward Smoke. "Let's get these bindings off."

There was the sound of a moan from Libs and then the view of Cutter skewed sideways. Then the screen, for lack of a better word, went black and stayed black.

"What about Teddy?" Dom asked Libs, leaning close to her. "How did you get to him?"

Silence.

"Smoke?" Dom said urgently.

"We've lost her," Dairy said.

"Libs," Dom said, leaning close to her. "Keep her with us! We need to know where she is."

Libs moaned. The screen stayed black. Dom looked up at Aiden and shook his head.

"Damn it, Smoke," Aiden shouted, stepping away from Dairy. "Help us! We want to bring you home."

The image around the room flickered to life again. Teddy, beaten to an almost unrecognizable mess.

"A deal is a deal," Cutter said from off screen. "Although you're a fool for making it. Look at him. It's not even him, anymore."

"You wouldn't understand," Smoke said in a broken voice.

"What I understand," he said slowly, "—is that within that well-trained, beautiful, warrior's body of yours is the mind and the heart of a pathetic *woman.*" The word dripped with scorn. "You've got one minute. Starting now."

Teddy grew larger on the screen as Smoke moved closer to him. When he finally looked up and recognized her, the expression of love and grief in his face caused a painful lump form in my throat. Smoke looked down and we saw her body convulse with crying.

"One minute," Sirena whispered so softly that I barely heard it.

Smoke had crossed her arms in front of herself, and her sharp thumbnail worked frantically, cutting and digging at a spot on her inner arm, drawing blood. I chewed on a knuckle as she stopped and then finagled a tiny capsule from inside her arm. We watched her blood-slicked fingers as her head lowered. What we couldn't see was obvious. She put the capsule into her own mouth. Teddy's face loomed larger as she came close for a kiss.

"Goodbye," Libs whispered a moment later. "I love you."

Smoke stepped back.

"Did you get a good enough look at him?" Cutter asked darkly. "Because you've had only the merest taste of what can be done. You haven't begun yet to get the full flavor. And you don't want to."

"You're right," she replied in a flat voice. She turned and started back toward Cutter.

"Stick to your end of our bargain," he said with a surprising tenderness. "And I will keep you from any fur—" He broke off as his gaze lowered slightly and filled with alarm. "What have you done?"

She looked down at herself. Although her left hand covered the wound on her right arm, blood had seeped around her fingers. Cutter yanked her hand away.

"Sir!" A male voice boomed from off-screen. "The prisoner!"

In a sickening whirl of motion, Teddy was back on full screen. He was dead – and he was vanishing.

He was gone.

I realized I'd been holding my breath and released it in a rush.

Cutter grabbed Smoke. "What have you done? This changes everything! Don't you—"

The image on screen skewed and faded. We saw only a ceiling and part of a wall.

"She's ingested something!" Cutter called. "Get her into the tank and hurry! I want her back."

Black screen. We waited, but it stayed black.

Aiden sighed. "Fuck," he said under his breath. "Get Lexy back," he said. "Our Smoke's cleared out."

"Libs," Dom said, cupping her face. "It's okay. Come on back. Come on back, baby girl."

Sirena nudged me. She headed for the door, which she opened before we reached it. I followed her out and down the hall, but after only a short distance, she stopped and leaned against the wall.

"Are you okay?" I asked.

She shook her head and then began to sob uncontrollably.

I pulled her close and held her. I was about to tell her it was okay, but it wasn't. What we'd just seen proved that everything was not okay. Everything, in fact, was pure shit.

18

Down Time

Sirena and I made our way back to her lodge. We were weak and needed sustenance. We also needed some down time after what we'd witnessed. She went into the kitchen to fix us a drink, and I stood in front of a fire in the hearth with my mind on Teddy and Smoke. She had ingested some of the poison, but had it been enough to kill her? If so, she was already dead. If not, they would make her pay for freeing Teddy. She'd made a fool of Cutter. I stared at the flames that emanated from rocks. "What is it that you burn in the hearth?" I asked, wanting to distract myself from the gruesome thoughts.

"Firerocks," she said as she came toward me with two steaming mugs. "It's mostly graphite. A little anthracite." She handed a mug over.

I gladly accepted. The warmth of it felt good in my hands. "Thank you."

"You're welcome."

I sipped. It was mildly sweet and creamy. "It's good. What is it?"

"White tea, almond cream and other spices," she said as she went toward a curved love seat. She sat.

I came and sat next to her, shifting to face her.

"If I shared the recipe," she said "You could make it at home and then you might not come here anymore."

"That is true. Because the recipe for this is exactly what I've been after."

A corner of her mouth quirked. "So now I know."

The teasing was a nice momentary diversion.

"It's so strange I don't feel any strain having you here, as long as it's been."

"Yeah," I said reluctantly. "About that."

She looked wary. "What?"

"I was shot."

Her eyes widened with alarm. "What?"

"I know. It's crazy."

"What are you talking about?"

"I was at school—"

"School?"

I nodded.

She seemed baffled. "How long do you go to school in your world?"

"Most go through high school, so that's twelve years. Then there's higher education. That could be another two years or four years or more depending on the degree you want."

She blinked, stymied by this notion.

"Anyway, this demented girl, I mean a real psychopath, came into school with a gun. Two actually, maybe more, I don't know." It felt unreal as I recounted it, more like a scene in a movie I'd seen than something that had occurred earlier that day. I took a sip. "I was hit."

"Tell me everything," she said with an intense frown.

"Okay. There's this really messed up girl who's involved with, well, murders."

She blinked. "The murders you mentioned when you first came here?"

I nodded. "Yes. She's part of this group which has mostly been caught. Unfortunately, she got away. But then … I saw her at school. She walked by the room I was in with a gun in hand. I just happened to be looking." *Because of a girl sneaking gummy worms.* I suddenly remembered the girl offering me one. I wondered what she thought now after everything that had happened. She'd probably always remember that she offered me a gummy worm, and then I freaked and left and all the rest of it happened. I shook my head. "I couldn't believe it. I got up and I followed her."

She huffed. "Why would you follow her?" she asked angrily.

162

"I thought I was supposed to," I said haltingly. "It's like I was led to do it, because I've had dreams and, uh, visions ... I'd guess you'd call them. And I found myself in the right places at the right times to learn things that turned out to be critical." I paused, noticing the tears pooled in her eyes. "Why does all that happen if there's not a bigger picture? I thought maybe it was my destiny."

She looked away to collect herself. "So you followed her. Go on."

I cocked my head. Was she pissed at me? "I don't mean it to sound all bad ass because that's not how it was," I assured her. "I was scared out of my mind, but I got to the room she was in. She'd herded all the kids and the teacher to the front of the room, and she was sitting on a desk facing them, having a good time scaring them shitless. I was hoping to sneak in from behind and grab her or the gun, but ... she saw me."

Sirena released a shaky breath. "And she shot you?"

I nodded. "I remember being knocked backwards and then staring up at the ceiling. I couldn't breathe."

"Where were you hit? Do you know?"

I shook my head. I remembered seeing the gun come up, the explosion. But the impact? I knew there was one and I'd felt it, but I couldn't pinpoint where I'd been hit. "It all happened so fast. I was knocked flat on my back. I couldn't breathe. I pictured all these faces of people I know. I thought of you, and the next thing I knew I was with you and Gabe."

She reached over and took hold of my hand. "I was upset," she said. Her eyes were pink rimmed from crying, but she was so damned beautiful. "Scared out of my mind. Was that how you put it? I hadn't been that close to a raid in a long time. To see that kind of violence and anguish—" She took a breath and exhaled. "I wished you were there. And then I felt you arc toward me, so I did the same and ... there you were. But I *knew* something was wrong."

For a moment, the magnitude of our connection overwhelmed me. "I didn't know up from down for a minute," I said. "I also don't know how bad things got back there. I don't even know if I was killed."

"No," she stated with a shake of her head. "You were not."

"You say that with such certainty."

"I am certain. You couldn't have died there, because you're here."

I thought about it. "Is it possible," I began.

"What?" she urged.

"I was shot and then I …bridged over here, but then my body died back there. You know what I'm saying? My energy, my spirit came here—"

She was shaking her head. "No. The spirit is connected to a physical manifestation. To our bodies. Once the body is destroyed, the spirit is drawn to another plane. If you had died back there, you couldn't be here."

I squeezed her hand, hoping she was right. "Sometimes I wish I was here. That I could be here all the time."

"I wish so, too. But it can't be."

"You mean, we don't know the way right now," I said.

She shook her head slowly. "Matt," she breathed. "In the eight centuries that have lapsed between your world and mine, we have learned to harness and manipulate our energy. It travels ahead and then the body catches up. But it is temporary. We are tied to a fixed time."

"Unless you find a wormhole and lock onto it," I said. After all, someone had done that. Daniel, aka Cres Singledon had done that.

She got up. "Let's eat," she said, offering me a hand up. "The night is not over."

I followed her into her kitchen and to an oddly shaped island. "May I help?" I offered. "I'm used to fending for myself."

"Here, we fend for each other, but I've got it this time. Thank you, though."

I sat in a chair and then gasped as it began to move and conform to me. "Whoa! My chair's alive."

She grinned and I saw her dimples. "Not alive. The sensors detect where you need support. You might feel stimulation, too."

I watched her with fascination as she worked. "How old were you when you came here?"

"Thirteen," she said without looking up. "They'd don't usually take anyone that young, but I'd lost my family in a raid. And I had abilities."

"I'm sorry about your family."

She glanced up at me. "Tell me about yours."

"It's just me and my mom."

She stopped chopping and looked up at me. "What's she like?"

I've always loathed that question, because I find her really difficult to describe. So are my feelings for her. I mean, I love her, of course, but she's more of a kid than I am. She's self-centered and sloppy and inconsiderate, but anytime I start to really dislike her, she turns everything on its ear. She defends me or she does that once-in-a-blue-moon unselfish thing, or she says something magnificent. "She's her own person," I hedged, settling for my old standby. "So is everyone part of a tier?"

"No. Hardly anyone is. It takes strong abilities to get accepted into training and then you have to excel at every level. And *then* you have to find a psylink or a psyleague."

"Okay, so a psylink is—"

She looked at me with solemnity. "Someone you share an almost total psychological connection with. Psylinks both bolster and feed off of one another's gifts. It's rare and very precious."

"Are Smoke and Teddy psylinks?"

"No. They're enleague. It's similar, but the connection is not as complete. It's strong, of course. It has to be." She put everything she'd chopped into a bowl and rubbed it on the surface in a circular motion. The surface under the bowl began to glow with heat. "Some of the most gifted people never get inducted into a tier, because they don't find the right circuit or

165

counterparts to connect to. They can still take part in the resistance, but not as part of a tier."

"The tiers, though, the best assignments go to them?"

"Usually. Because there's strength in numbers. Not counting CA's, maybe."

"What are CA's?"

"Counter assassins. They go after the Foundation's assassins."

"Assassins who go after assassins?"

She nodded. "I tried to get into the program, but I was judged to be too compassionate. They said my empathy would deter success." She selected glasses and poured a bubbling whitish drink from a small tapped barrel.

"What is it?" I asked as she handed me one.

She gave me a look. "Water."

It didn't taste as carbonated as it looked, but it was slightly tangy. "What's the huntress classified as? Is she a CA?"

"Who?"

"The huntress."

She shook her head. "I don't know of anyone who goes by that. Is she supposed to be one of us?"

"No, she's more like a mercenary."

"I have never heard of her. I also don't know of any mercenaries. Not here."

That was interesting when everything and everyone else in the game had been based on truth and real people. "So, Teddy and Smoke are Tier 5," I said, recalling what Smoke said.

"Yes. Along with Ji, Glass and Ocean."

"Is tier one is the best?"

"Not the best. It's the tier that's been in existence the longest." She dished the food onto two plates and slid one in front of me before coming around to sit next to me.

"This looks great. Who knew you were a good cook?"

"Is that not mentioned in the game?"

I smiled. It felt so good and natural to be with her. "Back to the subject. Let's say I was here and went into training. Let's say I was good enough and psylinks were found. So then I'm paired up with, what? Four other people?"

It took her a moment to respond. "A tier has a minimum of four people, but there can be as many as eight."

"Do some people find two and three psylinks?"

"No! Psylinks are rare. Members of a tier are psyleagues. They have synchronicity. Each member of a particular tier is able to get in sync with every other member of that tier. In a crowded room, one of them might think, 'Look at me,' and all the others would simultaneously receive the thought and look."

"Ah."

"Everyone is tested for ability and then you're tested several more times to find connections."

"Like puzzle pieces coming together. That must be so cool."

She smiled quizzically. "Some of your phrases are strange to me."

I watched her toy with the last of her food. "Were you ever in a tier?"

She didn't look up. "Yes."

I'd felt her defenses come up. Should I not have asked?

She looked up at me. "I know you just want to understand." She leaned back with a sigh and her chair closed around her as if giving her a hug. "There were five of us. But there was an explosion and three of us were killed."

I felt a hollowness swell in my chest, an echo of her sorrow. "I'm sorry."

She nodded.

"How long ago?"

"A year and a half."

I nodded slowly. "How is it that you and I are psylinks?"

She shrugged. "We just are."

We looked at each other, seconds ticked by and then we both got up and began cleaning the dishes to keep ourselves in check. "There's a lav there," she said. "And one through the bedroom."

"Thanks." I did need to use it. "You know that mind reading thing is probably going to get me in serious trouble one of these days," I said as I walked away.

I felt her answering laugh. "It wasn't mind reading."

When I went back downstairs, Sirena was standing at the open front door, staring out at the night. I leaned against the opposite door jamb. "Should we go back and check on them?"

"Soon," she said quietly. She turned toward me. "You can lie down, if you want," she said shyly.

Whoa, the way my heart began racing. "If I did," I said. "And if I could convince you to lie down next to me, I wouldn't want to get up again, and I know you want to go back and check on the others."

She sighed and nodded.

"Do you think Smoke is still alive?" I asked.

"Yes. They want information from her."

"But the poison—"

She shook her head. "Not enough to kill. That takes the whole capsule."

"You know she's in the maze. Right? So why can't someone go after her?"

"Because they'd have us tagged as soon as we were scanned."

"What does that mean?"

"Surely there's a database of criminals in your world."

"Okay, yeah."

"Anytime they want to, an officer of the Foundation can scan anyone that they want to. That raid we saw?"

I nodded.

"They randomly haul in people, young and old, hoping to catch one of us or anyone with rebel intel."

"How is a person scanned?"

"Facial recognition, handprints, DNA, mind probes. They have a registry of every inhabitant."

"I could go in. I'm not registered."

Her eyes widened with alarm. "What? No!"

"Why?"

"How could you even ask that after what we saw? You don't even know this world."

"Right. I'm not officially one of you. Why would there be any point in hurting an innocent?"

"They do it all the time! My family was innocent. You don't understand how evil they are. The very fact that you're not registered means you're *illegal*. That's grounds for deportment or even execution."

"Okay. I'm sorry. I didn't mean to upset you."

She took a breath, shook her head and exhaled slowly. "It's upsetting to be helpless. Unless we can find a way to hone in on her exact location and somehow dematerialize and extract her, it's over. And that's probably not possible because of the containment field they've built. I know you want to help, but it's not possible."

"Okay. All right," I soothed. "Just one or two more questions?"

"Of course. Yes. Ask."

"What's RU 2? Smoke said she was stationed at RU 2."

"It's here. Where we were earlier. It stands for Rebel Unit. Ours was the second one formed."

"And what's DEC?" I asked, remembering something else Smoke said.

"Someone with the ability to dematerialize and evanesce on their own and who can communicate telepathically."

"Evanesce?"

"Vanish and reappear."

"Smoke can do that?"

She looked as if I was missing some basic fact. "Yes, but not in the maze."

"Can you do that, too?"

"Yes."

My breath caught. "Is that what we're doing when we bridge from one world to another?"

She shook her head. "Bridging is where two energies connect to get from place to place. That's easier than evup." She stepped closer and kissed me lightly. "We should go check in."

I liked the sound of we. I liked the feeling of we. "'Kay."

19

The Maze

"It's undetectable," Ji stated half an hour later as he held up a tracker/transmitter the size of a button of a dress shirt. "Look at it."

At least a dozen people were involved in a discussion about whether I should be placed in the path of raid, which might mean a trip into the maze. The Resistance had at least one mole inside the ranks of the Foundation, so they knew about some of the raids. It probably wouldn't be difficult to get swept up.

I had made the suggestion to Ji, which had drawn an immediate and really unhappy response from Sirena, but only because she was being protective. It didn't seem that much of a risk when I wasn't known to the Foundation. Ji assure me they could provide me with impeccable fake credentials.

"No!" Sirena said again. It was her unwavering stance on the matter.

"We give him a clean ID attached to an undesirable sector," Aiden pondered aloud. "Chances are, they'll sweep him up and right back out."

"It's the 'chances are' part I have a problem with," Sirena seethed.

"Do you memorize well?" a guy asked me.

"I do," I replied. They were the first words I'd spoken since making the suggestion.

"You'll have to memorize an I.I. number, a cover name and an address," Dom spoke up.

"What's an I.I. number?"

"I brought him here," Sirena said. "And I say no!" She was alone in her dissenting position and growing increasingly emotional because of it. "He's not ready."

"An Inhabitant Identity number," Dom replied. "Assigned at either birth or relocation when a profile is started."

"Seery," Dairy spoke up. "Think! His innocence makes him perfect. It's what keeps him safe. I say yes."

"Yes," Ji agreed.

"Yes," Aiden said.

Yes was called out several more times, which prompted Sirena to object. "What about the brain scanners? He doesn't know how to block thoughts."

"Um, actually," I spoke up, "I blocked my intention to bring the subject up from you. I knew you'd want to stop me."

"Get him ready," Aiden ordered.

Sirena grabbed my arm in a panic, so I let her lead me off to the side. "I want to do this," I said quietly enough that only she could hear.

She was close to tears. "No. I don't like it," she said beseechingly.

"I know," I said calmly.

"If you get hurt—"

"I won't."

"Matt," she pleaded.

I leaned in and touched my forehead to hers, wrapping my hand around the back of her neck. I almost became intoxicated with her scent, which had flared with the surging of her emotions. I want to do something worthy," I admitted. "If I ever have a chance to stay—"

When I pulled away, her expression was searching and then she nodded. Reluctantly. I was relieved we were finally on the same page. It's the only place I ever want to be. "I loved you before I even met you."

She gave me a sad smile. "We knew each other well before we met."

"Come on, loverboy," Dairy said. "Lots of instruction to go through. Including mind blocking," she added, giving Sirena a significant look.

I started toward Dairy, and Sirena stayed close by my side.

"I'll generate a clean number," Ji said. "Here," he said, handing Dairy the transmitter before going in the opposite direction.

"Besides your number," Aiden said as he walked alongside us, "—you may be asked your place of residence and what you were doing when they grabbed you. Tell them you were going to meet a girl. Keep your answers short. Don't volunteer anything. Just answer their questions as briefly as possible and follow instructions. Hopefully, you'll walk in and back out. Even that will help. Except for the snatch we got from Libs and Smoke today, we haven't gotten any reconnaissance into the maze for a long time."

"Anytime you want out," Sirena spoke up, "—until you're actually in the maze, we can extract you."

"But once you're inside, they'll have to release you," Dairy added.

I nodded. "I understand. Should I have some naira, just in case?"

Aiden gripped my arm and came to a halt, as did the rest of us. "This is no game, Matthew," he stated, his gaze piercing.

Had I sounded flippant? I hadn't meant to. "I know that."

"We're going to keep this simple," Aidan said. "Get fed into the system and shit back out. You don't need naira. We don't have time to train you."

"What if I encounter Smoke?"

His eyes flashed. "You won't."

"But just say by some crazy, remote possibility—"

"You won't! She's in the bowels of the maze under more surveillance than you can possibly imagine."

"Still," Dairy mused.

"Still what?" Aiden snapped at her.

"Why can't he have something if we can hide it on him well enough?"

"Because everything we give him puts him at greater risk," one of the twins reasoned having just joined us.

"That's right," Aiden seconded.

"I think he should have it," Sirena spoke up.

Dairy nodded. "One of those wafers could be slipped into a flap on the inside the bottom of his sleeve."

"Matt, you don't have to do this," the twin said to me. "I don't see what good it could do that's worth risking your neck."

"It's already decided," Dairy said to him.

"I wasn't here to get a vote," he retorted. "And neither was Gabe."

"There are only two of us of dissenting opinion," Sirena said to Westin.

"And you're with me now," I spoke up, directing it to her. "Right?"

"Of course, I'm with you," she replied passionately. "I still don't want you to go."

"He can have the naira," Aiden decided. "If it can be done fast enough."

Dairy wiggled the fingers of her outstretched hand at me. "Give me your shirt."

Westin shook his head. "He's proven his value already and he's only just gotten here."

"Yes, he's proven his value," Dairy replied hotly. "And he wants to keep on. Just like you. Just like me."

"They didn't ask me to do this," I said to Westin. "I volunteered. I want to do it." I took off my shirt and handed it to Dairy and she walked off with it.

"So, that's that?" Westin asked.

"That's that," Aiden confirmed. He smacked my arm. "Come on. We've got work to do. I sure as fuck don't need you on my conscience."

~~~

Second thoughts came fast and furiously as I was caught in the electronic field. It buzzed and crackled , ruffling my hair and skin even through my clothes. It was painful and scary as hell. It occurred to me that, at any second, the person behind the controls, whomever or whatever they were, could up the juice and we would literally be fried. Every single one of us unfortunate enough to be trapped would be burnt toast, laying blackened and stiff with smoke rising from our lifeless bodies.

Once you're caught, you're caught, but that didn't stop the panic and pandemonium. It didn't stop people from trying to get away, even knowing they couldn't. FO's were shouting, people were crying and occasionally screaming and writing in pain because the more you resist, the more it hurts. I stood as still as a statue, except for the rapid breathing and trembling.

When the force eased up, we were herded into one of the conveyances I'd seen before. Inside was subway car-like, but with no place to sit and nothing to hang onto. The yellow glow messed with my eyes. The transport took off slowly and then picked up enough speed that, when it stopped, it threw us off balance. A few people fell.

The thing jerked hard a couple of times and then began lowering into the ground like a massive elevator, casting us into darkness. The only light came from the yellow light from the ceiling panels. It seemed as if there was less oxygen than before, but that may have been sheer panic on my part. I felt rails connect when we'd reached a platform and then we started moving forward again.

No one looked at anyone else. It occurred to me that, in the way tragedy causes strangers to connect, fear seems to cause the opposite reaction, a disconnect. The one exception was a woman clinging to the hand of a small boy. Even with long bangs partly covering her eyes, I could tell she was watching me with great intensity. She started toward me. "Are you clean?" she whispered when she reached me.

She had to mean my I.I. number. I nodded stiffly.

"Will you take him? Please?"

I experienced a whole new kind of fear. "What?"

"They'll tag me," she said under her breath. "They'll tag me and hurt him. That's what they do, to make you talk. Please!"

I looked down at the boy, who was maybe four years old, and then back up at her. I could feel her fear. She was eaten up with it, nauseous with it. "How do know they'll tag you?"

"Because I know," she replied beseechingly. A tear rolled down her face. "I beg you."

"I haven't done this before," I said slowly and as quietly as I could. "They might tag me, too."

"They won't. You'll be fine," she stated flatly. "I'm a precog," she whispered.

I blinked as the significance of the statement hit home. "Is that how you know?"

She looked off, her lips trembled and her shoulders hunched inward. No wonder she was eaten up with fear. "Will he be okay with me?"

She nodded again. "We've told him it's like a game where he pretends not to know me or his father." More tears fell and wiped them away with her free hand. "He understands. As well as he can."

The car jerked onto a new set of rails, sending everyone careening a few steps.

"I don't know if they got my husband," she continued when we'd regained our footing. "We were at the night market. It's been safer, but then they were there. Everywhere. We all ran, but—"

I knew because I'd experienced it. I'd had the advantage of knowing what would happen and it had still been terrifying. The car jerked to a stop, sending us forward a step yet again.

"We're close now," she said. "I've done this before." Visibly shaking, she leaned down and hugged her son. I experienced a severe bout of dizziness as everything around me went into slow motion.

Tell her to fall back. Get off the transport and fall back.

The woman stood, poised to walk away, but I grabbed hold of her arm. "Get off this thing," I said breathlessly. "But hang back. Work your way to the back of the group. Don't be obvious. Try not to be seen."

She drew back slightly and studied me, too shocked to speak. Then she nodded and I felt a pulsating of hope from her. Was she glimpsing a new outcome?

The ride was at an end. Doors opened, and we were jostled as people pushed forward. The woman stepped into flow of traffic which is when it occurred to me that I'd never learned her name. Or the boy's. I squatted beside him, ignoring the crush of legs around us. "I'm Luka," I said, using my newly assigned alias. It came pretty easily. "What's your name?"

"Michael," he replied solemnly.

"Okay, Michael. We're going to pretend that we're brothers. Are you a good pretender?"

He nodded.

"Me, too," I said. "Ever had a big brother before?"

"No," he said in a small voice that made me want to scoop him up and protect him with everything I had. I knew my friends at RU2 could get me out of there. Could they get us both out? Was that the responsible thing to do? It was one thing to put myself at risk, but a whole other thing to take a child along for the ride. Still, if Michael's mother had been telling the truth, and I sensed she had been, I would be okay. She'd been so sure that she'd entrusted her child to a stranger's care. "I never had a little brother before either, but we'll be fine."

Michael clutched his fisted hands to his chest, and I felt a squeeze in my chest. I stood back up, offered my hand, and he slipped his into it. I took a deep breath and we filed out of the bus. Outside, in the chilly night air, we were directed toward a massive building. It looked like black marble or granite. Overly bright, greenish-white lights on tall poles bleached all color from our skin. I looked back for Michael's mother, but I didn't see her. I looked at the people in front of us. Even though they almost all had their backs to me, I could tell she was not among them. I nodded to myself. That was good.

The process inside the facility was disturbingly organized. People faced forward in long, slowly moving lines. We were directed into a line, and we went. Obeying wasn't hard. The instinct for survival meant instant compliance. Not only was fear was thick in the air, it seeped through to the core with the aim of a heat-seeking missile. Michael stayed by my side, his hand in mine, stepping when I stepped. Midway through the line, I squatted beside him. "Our last name is Redding," I said quietly. "So, your name is Michael Redding. Okay?"

He nodded.

"Do you remember my name?"

"Luka."

I nodded and gave him an encouraging smile before standing back up.

From somewhere in the cavernous structure, a man's voice rang out. "But why?" he cried, his shrill voice echoing eerily. "I've done nothing." He suddenly screamed, although the sound was cut off quickly.

I pulled Michael closer. I saw the man's limp body being dragged away by uniformed officials.

"Where's my mama?" Michael asked. He'd begun crying.

I picked him up and he buried his face against my neck. I let him cry, stroking his back. "Your mom is strong and smart. Right?" I asked quietly.

He nodded.

"That's right. So she'll be fine. We'll all be fine. You and I will get out of here and you'll go back home, and you'll forget all about this. You just have to believe it."

When we neared the front of the line, I hoped Michael would just keep his head down, because the beings at the head of the line were scary as hell. I'd seen them on screen, compliments of Smoke and Libs, but up close, they were way bigger than I'd thought and they had a pungent odor. Their glassy-eyed gaze locked onto each subject as they performed a mind scan. I'd been told that it felt like having your brain combed. I'd also been assured that it could be blocked.

I'd been instructed to relax and visualize myself shielded by a diamond casing that nothing could penetrate. Of all the learning, cramming and repeating I'd done, shielding had taken the longest. It had taken until Sirena acknowledged I could do it. Not only could I do it, I was doing it. Michael and I were safe behind thick, diamond walls. I was looking at the alien sons of bitches through the diamond. I could see them, and they could see us, but they couldn't touch us. Not me and not Michael. They could not read me. They could not know me.

"Name?" an FO asked.

"Redding. Luka Redding and this is my brother Michael."

The creature locked in on me, compelling me to look at it. I did. I watched its eyes go from yellow to brown. As they changed, I became calmer and more removed. *I'm inside a diamond casing where nothing can touch me. Not me and not Michael.*

"Number?" the FO asked.

"86304-78.25," I replied.

The FO glanced down at a device in his hand and gave a curt nod. "Haud gravitas." I recognized the phrase. It was Latin for not important or of no importance or something like that. I hadn't loved Latin, but I'd retained some of it. The FO glanced at the alien who was still studying me with an unfathomable expression. "Well?" he demanded impatiently.

The psychic reader gave a flat slashing motion, and the FO gestured for us to move. "Next!"

It was over. *Oh, my God,* the relief! I walked blindly, following others outside and toward a slowing filling conveyance for the return home. "We're okay," I told Michael. "We're going home, now."

"Will Mama be there?"

I put him down. "I hope so." We stepped up and onto the conveyance. Then Michael gasped and tugged at me.

"That's my dad," he whispered excitedly.

I followed Michael's gaze to the emotionally wrecked face of his father. The resemblance was unmistakable. I let go of his hand.

Michael took off, which was fine since no one was paying the least bit of attention to us. I watched the father pick his son up and hold him close. The man nodded at me with tears shining in his eyes. "Thank you," he mouthed.

I nodded back and then turned away. My arms suddenly felt too light, as if part of me was missing. I couldn't fathom how terrible it would be to have your child hurt in front of you to make you talk. It was unconscionable. Evil. Suddenly, I knew what I needed to do. I was on borrowed time, anyway, so I got back off the vehicle.

"What do you think you're doing?" an FO demanded.

He wasn't the only one asking. Sirena and I'm not sure who else were going crazy.

"Is it possible," I began, but my voice faltered. I cleared my throat. "I'd like to speak with Cutter."

The man scoffed. "Would you now?"

"I would. Please."

"Why?"

"It's personal," I stammered.

"Are you a pigeon?"

I hesitated. "I can't really say." He pointed out an FO stationed outside one of the entrances to the building, and I pressed a hand to my thigh and walked.

"What?" a different FO snapped.

"I'm to see Cutter," I said, trying to sound convincing.

Matt, stop it! Get out of there!

The man reached into a pouch and handed me a square of what looked like clear plastic. "That way," he said, pointing to a different door than we'd used before. "Take it to a desk."

Inside, at one of the dozen manned desks, my I.I. number was programmed onto the square. "Put it on and make sure it's visible at all times," the woman behind the desk instructed me as she handed it back. "Who are you to see?"

"Cutter."

She pointed me to the next checkpoint. With the pass stuck to my shirt, I explained less and less as I went. I was finally escorted onto one of the glass elevator cars by a guard with a body odor issue, and we went down I don't know how many levels. When it stopped, the car moved laterally. The place was enormous. It was a city. Between the fast movement, my frayed nerves and the odor of my escort, I felt sick by the time the doors opened.

I followed the guard out and saw Cutter himself standing there, apparently having been summoned. I think my blood chilled a few degrees.

"What is this?" Cutter asked the guard irritably.

"They said to bring him to you," the man stammered. I wasn't the only one who was nervous.

Cutter narrowed his eyes. "Why?"

"I ... wasn't—"

Cutter lifted his hand and the man stopped speaking, and then Cutter turned his dark gaze on me. It was my turn to speak but, for a second, my vocal apparatus totally failed. "I wanted—" This had been a mistake. A horrendous mistake. I'd be hurt if not killed and Sirena would be devastated.

"You were saying," Cutter said coldly.

I couldn't utter a word.

"You wanted ... what? To invite me home for dinner? To share rebel intelligence? To become my apprentice?"

I nodded. "Yes, sir."

He looked furious. "I was summoned here for this?" he demanded of the guard.

The guard cleared his throat. "I'll take him back, sir. Or to wherever you say. He'll be punished."

"How did you happen to ask for me?" Cutter asked me.

Not only was my voice failing me, my legs were nearly mutinying, as well. Soon I'd be a pile of blubbering flesh, unable to speak, run or anything. As if running would do any good. "Your name," I managed to say. "Everyone knows your name."

Cutter's top lip curled and then he looked back at the guard with expressionless eyes. "Go."

I felt a piercing stab of fear in my heart. In a matter of seconds, the elevator door closed again and the guard was gone. He didn't wait to be told twice.

Cutter eyed me critically. "What does everyone *know* about me? Besides my name."

"That you're one of the top officials," I stammered.

"False. What else?"

"Just that you have power."

"And you want power?"

"It's better than not having any."

"What's your name?"

"Matt," I blurted without thinking. I realized I'd screwed up immediately but tried not to react.

"Do you know what we do here, Matt?"

I racked my brain for the best possible reply.

"Oh, come now," he said. "You must have an idea."

"You try and find rebels," I replied haltingly.

Slowly, he smiled. "Did you ever think of becoming a rebel?"

I shifted on my feet. If I lied to him, he'd know. "When I was younger."

"Did they ever approach you?"

"No."

"Did you ever try to find them?"

I opened my mouth then shut it.

He shrugged. "I can see where it might have a certain appeal to a restless young man. You shouldn't feel too badly about the rejection. They don't just take anyone. It's quite an elite group. They all have some talent of significance. Do you have any talent?" Without waiting for a response, he turned and started off. Not knowing what else to do, I followed, keeping a few steps behind.

"That was the guard who reeked, I hope?"

"Yes, sir."

"So, you want to be my apprentice, do you?"

"I don't know that I would have put it like that," I hedged.

He stopped and turned to face me.

"I wanted to find out about working here, and yours was the only name I knew. I didn't really think I'd get to you."

"Ah. Boys and their dares. Young men and their brazenness. Let me guess. You're alone in the world. No money, no future, no real direction."

I didn't reply.

"You were entranced by the idea of joining the rebels, but they aren't interested in you, so why not see what the other side has to offer? In fact, why not ask for me."

I shifted on my feet. "I'm sorry I bothered you. I can see it was a mistake."

"Can you?"

I nodded. "Yes, sir."

"Are you no longer curious to see if you have what it takes to a member of the Foundation?"

I swallowed and shook my head. "I'm really sorry to have bothered you."

"But not as sorry as you will be, I think."

My stomach knotted with trepidation. I might have taken off in a dead run if there had been any chance of escape.

"I had a brother named Mathias," Cutter remarked. "Are you a Mathias?"

I shook my head as best I could; my neck muscles were so tight. "Matthew."

"Come, Matthew."

As if I had a choice at this point. As I trudged on, I saw a pair of ominous looking black doors beyond the end of the hall. Just before we reached them, he stopped and turned back to me. One hall had emptied onto another, which ran in the opposite direction, and he glanced in both directions before speaking again. "I rarely do anything beneficial for anyone else," he said quietly. "The last time I tried, earlier today, as a matter of fact, it backfired and now there are consequences."

I knew what he was talking about but couldn't let on. If I could just find a way to ask about her. Ask whether she was alive or dead.

"What would it mean to work here, do you think?"

I wasn't sure if he meant what it would mean to me personally or what might the work entail. "I don't know."

"But you want to know," he said.

I couldn't bring myself to respond. Something was up and it was something not good. It had to do with going through those black doors.

"Bear one thing in mind," Cutter said as he reached out and gripped my shoulder. "Sometimes a favor may not feel like a favor." He grabbed hold of my arm, opened one of the doors and marched me through.

The noise hit first. Sounds of pain and misery. The sight took longer to comprehend. I knew people were hanging, but their figures were wrong, distorted. It was because they were hanging in strange positions, some upside down by one or both ankles, some from their wrists, but with their arms behind them, their body weight pulling, tearing shoulder muscles and tendons. Meanwhile, FO's meandered amongst them. I shuddered violently. It was sickening. Horrible.

"Cutter," a guard called genially. "What brings you to the meat locker? Need a slab?"

Sickening. Vile. Horrible. *Evil.* "Oh, my God," I muttered under my breath. I was going to be sick.

"Touring," Cutter stated coolly.

"Who's this with you? One of yours or one for us?"

I started hyperventilating. I saw starbursts. I became aware of powerful hands on my arm and back and knew I was being dragged somewhere. *They would hang me now, too.* The next thing I knew, I was back in the hall, crouching on the floor, my back against the wall. Cutter's hands were on my wrists, his face close to mine. He was commanding me to breathe slowly. I tried, but people were being tortured not twenty feet from where I sat! *Tortured.* Aiden had been right. This was no game. It was no fucking game. Who had made a game of such a sick, evil regime?

"I said breathe slowly," Cutter repeated sternly.

I managed to finally get a grip and my dizziness lessened.

Cutter let go of me and stood. "Who said, 'Power tends to corrupt, and absolute power corrupts absolutely?'"

I didn't reply. I couldn't even think straight.

"Get up," he ordered. Apparently, I took too long so he reached down and pulled me up. "That was not a rhetorical question."

"I don't know who said it." I'd heard it, but I didn't know who'd said it. All I knew was that my every limb was quaking, and tears were way too close for comfort.

"Then guess."

My mind raced. "Churchill?"

"No. Listen. 'Power tends to corrupt, and absolute power corrupts absolutely. Great men are almost always bad men.'"

I shook my head. I didn't know who'd said it, and what difference did it fucking make anyway?

"A man named John Acton said it many centuries ago," Cutter stated. "Lord Acton. Remember that next time I ask you, or you will spend an hour of observation in there," he nodded angrily toward the door. "It may not be the longest hour of your life, but you will think it is."

I shook my head slowly. "Why?"

"Why would I require you to do that?"

"Why are those people being tortured?" A tear slid down my face and I quickly wiped it away.

Cutter's eyes narrowed and he considered me in silence for several moments. "Why not?"

I gawked. Had a more terrible, more hateful response ever been uttered? These people were beyond monstrous.

"Still want to be one of us?"

"There's not even a reason, is there?" I couldn't shake the images of that room. Somehow, we had to get back here and free those people. Never before had I grasped what it would be like to charge into battle knowing you might well be forfeiting your life for the sake of something more important than yourself, but I got it now. No matter what the personal cost, some things were worth it. "You don't even care," I accused.

"Would it matter if I did? And since you cannot possibly know the answer to that, allow me to provide it. No. Not in the least," he added, enunciating sharply.

Something internal warned me to stop. Was that Sirena's voice in my mind? "But you have the power."

He cocked his head and his expression changed. I felt like he was looking right through me. "You don't belong here. Do you?"

I hesitated, but then shook my head. "No."

"And yet you waltzed right in here. Asked to see me. Which takes the act beyond brazenness. Suicidal, perhaps? Are you suicidal?"

"No."

"You do realize I could do anything with you I wanted? Including have you hung back there. At the snap of a finger."

I didn't move a muscle or respond in any way. Unless, maybe, the terror that I felt came shining through, which is not unlikely.

"I won't. Which makes this your lucky day. Do you feel it?"

"Do I feel lucky?" I stammered, wanting to make sure I got the question right.

He nodded.

I swallowed. "I think I will when I walk out of here."

"Oh, I imagine you will. As you should. You *foolish* boy," he finished heatedly. He took a deep breath and exhaled. "What was the quote I shared earlier?"

"'Power tends to corrupt, and absolute power corrupts absolutely. Great men are almost always bad men.' Lord Acton."

"Remember it."

"I won't forget it." And I meant it. I knew then and there that what I'd just witnessed would be something I'd never be able to forget. Lord Acton's quote would forever be accompanied by the memory of people being tortured. It would forever be something that made me ache. Made me physically ill.

"Do you know, I resented the intrusion when I was told I had a visitor, but I do believe it may have done me some good. And it has certainly benefited you. Misguided, as you were." He started off again.

186

His pace was slower than it had been before, but I still struggled to keep up because my legs were so weak. We walked to what looked like an elevator door, but when we reached it, it slid open revealing another corridor. We passed through several more of these. I had no idea where we were going, but I hoped to God it was not to see anymore rooms of torture. "You said you had a brother," I said, hoping to get on some sort of personal level if that was possible. "Did he die?"

"Yes. A long time ago."

"I'm sorry."

"Don't be. People die. I barely remember him."

So much for getting personal. We approached an observation window and I experienced a powerful, zinging feeling even before we reached it and I saw Smoke inside. She was sitting on a chair in the middle of a small room, her feet shackled and her hands handcuffed behind her. Her face was bruised and swollen, her lip split open.

"I tried to help her, but she made it impossible," Cutter said as he watched her.

I could only stare. One of the supposedly undetectable things on me was a sort of GPS device, so the group now knew where Smoke was. I had the poison tablet, too. It was wafer thin, slightly larger than the size of a quarter sewn into a tiny pocket in my shirt.

"Very soon, she will fall back into other hands. I'll not get her back again."

I didn't trust myself to speak.

"She won't talk," he continued. "Which means she'll die. Slowly." He looked at me. "I've angered some people who will wish to demonstrate their moment of power by taking her interrogation to a level of brutality unlike anything you can imagine."

"Why show me this?"

He was quiet for a moment as he considered me. "There is a civility about you that's … affecting. Perhaps she'll respond to you. Go in there and convince her to cooperate with me. At least, to give the *illusion* of cooperation. I think you owe me that. Do you agree?"

I nodded jerkily.

"Convince her to talk *only* to me. They're coming for her. There's no stopping that. But when they come for her, she's to declare that she will speak only to me. They'll take her anyway. They'll try and break her but if she can hold out, I'll do what I can to save her." He studied me, his dark eyes glinting. "Is your name really Matthew?"

My heart had been beating hard before, but now it swelled and hammered and rocked my entire being. "Yes."

He glanced down at the square pass. "And if I run that identification?"

"It will come up as Luka Redding."

His eyes narrowed. "Why would you trust me? Of all people."

"I don't know," I admitted.

"Did you come for her?"

"I ... hoped."

"But you're not one of them, are you?"

"Only in spirit."

He considered this silently. "What they managed to pull off earlier—"

I nodded.

"You know?" he asked in a whisper.

Again, I nodded.

"Are you able to ... do the same?"

"I think so."

We heard a nearby door slam.

"Go," he ordered. "But know that whatever you say and do in there will be observed. You *do* want to walk of here today."

I quickly started forward despite my knees practically knocking. I opened the door and entered the room and stopped in front of the table. Smoke looked up at me as if she didn't recognize me. On second thought, there was hatred in her gaze, probably because she thought I was a traitor. There had been suspicion of me from the beginning and my being there now confirmed it for her. I pulled back a chair and sat across from her wondering how I was going to do what I needed to when we were being watched and her hands were restrained. "Cutter wants to help you," I said.

She remained expressionless. "Then he can uncuff my hands," she replied coolly.

The door opened and Cutter came in. "I can," he said. But what do I get in return besides trickery and deceit?"

Smoke's eyes stayed on mine as Cutter leaned close to uncuff her, his lips nuzzling her ear as he did so. Her face remained absolutely expressionless and her eyes did not waiver from mine. I used the time and the distraction to free the naira wafer. Cutter straightened, gave me a look and then walked back out.

Smoke looked down at her raw looking wrists and rubbed them. One of her eyes was beginning to swell shut. "What do you want?"

"Talk to Cutter. He wants to help you. Whatever it is you know, it's not worth dying over. It's not worth being tortured over."

Her head snapped up at me and the venom that surfaced in her froze me for a second.

"Get away from me before I scratch your eyes out!" She lunged forward and screamed the last of this.

I jerked back and then stood. I had the poison tablet in my fingers, but it would be seen if I put in on the table. Could I drop it? Leave it on the chair? *What?* No answers came. I'd been given the very chance I'd wanted and I was failing. Again. I'd made it that far and I was failing. "I'm sorry," I whispered.

"Sorry?" she breathed. She leaned slightly more forward, her hands on the table. "If there is still anything good or decent in you, leave this place. Now. Don't become one of them."

"Please," I said as I leaned forward and grabbed her hands, transferring the poison. "Just consider what—"

"Consider fucking yourself," she screamed, jerking away from me. *But she had the tablet!* I left the room, feeling sick from the tension. I half expected to see an angry mob hovering around the observation window, but only Cutter stood post. Immediately, he turned and walked away. I followed. When we reached an elevator, we got on and started up or over or down. Who even knew? It moved so fast, I couldn't see where we were going.

"You got it to her?" he asked.

"Yes."

"Leave this place and never come back."

I stared straight ahead and nodded. I wondered if Smoke was disappearing yet. I hoped so but if it happened too soon, would I make it out?

"However," Cutter added, "should you ever *accidentally* get detained, ask for me. Tell them you're my ... cousin."

I was so surprised, I couldn't reply, and then doors opened. A guard stood there.

"Escort him out," Cutter ordered coldly.

"With penalty, sir?"

"No. He has suffered his penalty."

The FO gestured me out. I stepped off and didn't look back, although I was tempted. I really wanted to see the expression on Cutter's face.

As I followed the guard to an exit, I kept expecting to be grabbed and arrested. And then tortured? What if they did that to me? How strong would I be? I thought of Teddy and what they'd done to him. I thought of Smoke and what she'd gone through. I wanted to be that strong and loyal, but was I?

Cutter and his damned quote. The quote that came back to me was, 'All it takes for evil to prevail is for good men to do nothing.' Although I didn't remember who'd said that one either. I pressed on the burning spot in the center of my stomach knowing that we had to get back there and help those people. No matter what.

I made it outside and breathed in the cool air deeply. It should have revived me. Instead, this all-consuming dizziness descended. I tried to fight it as I made my way toward the blurry, yellow-lighted square conveyance, but vertigo completely overwhelmed me and the night swallowed me whole.

20

Answers

It took unbelievable effort to open my eyes. When I
managed it, I found myself in a hospital room. I was hooked to
an IV while a heart monitor beeped proof that I had survived the
shooting. Mom sat next to the bed staring off in a daze. It was
obvious she'd been crying because her makeup was a disaster,
her face was red and blotchy. My mouth was so dry; I could
barely speak. "Mom?"

She looked at me and then jumped up. "Matty! Oh, Matty!"

I wanted to assure her I was okay, but it took too much
energy to speak.

She reached for the buzzer and began pressing it over and
over. "Oh, my God, I've been going out of my mind! You were
shot. Do you know you were shot?" She kept pressing the
button. "Oh, baby. I'm so glad you're awake."

"Hasom water?" It felt like my mouth was full of cotton.

"Yeah, yeah, yeah." She raised the head of my bed, and
then reached for a cup on the bedside table and helped me to
drink. "Where are those fucking doctors?" she said under her
breath.

"How many died?" I asked in a strained whisper. Tears
filled my eyes, but I didn't have the strength to fight them.

She looked stricken, but she shook her head. "No one! A
girl and another guy were shot, besides you, but no one was
killed. Because of you."

Was that true? I tried to think back, but everything was a
muddled mix. I remembered seeing Dora walk by in the hall,
and then seeing the girl in the red shirt. I flashed back on the
second I poked my head in the room where Dora had taken a
class hostage, and then the moment she turned on me. The gun

in her hand. I remembered seeing the gun. But the events in Ruaun3 were far clearer in my memory.

"You came into the room where … that person was, because you'd seen her with a gun." She wiped the corner of my mouth with the pad of her thumb. "She'd was going to kill them all, but you came in … and she shot you."

The sensation I was experiencing was what I imagine Alice of Alice-in-Wonderland felt when she drank the shrinking potion. I was fading and growing small. Mom kept talking and I tried to grasp the words.

"The teacher and some of the kids rushed her. They got the gun away, but she fought like the fuckin' maniac she is and that's when two other kids got shot. But no one died. You're hurt the worst."

But I'd heard gunfire from somewhere else in the school. Hadn't I? I wanted to ask about it, but I couldn't keep my eyes open.

"Matty, honey, stay awake."

I struggled to open my eyes again. I vaguely remember nurses and doctors rushing into the room, but that's all. When I woke again, it was dark outside. The hallway was bright and my door was partially open which provided enough light to see bunches of flowers and balloon arrangements. I saw colorful signs and big, cut out letters. MMM. *Oh, Geez.* Mother Matt Matthews. Like I'd ever live that down. I felt disappointed that I was alone and I had a powerful thirst. I tried to sit but couldn't. I reached for my water but knocked it over.

"I'm here," a familiar voice said.

Sirena. She righted the cup and refilled it. She raised the head of the bed up, sat next to me and helped me drink. She was naked but draped in a hospital blanket.

"How are you here?" I asked weakly. "When I didn't bridge you over?" I added to be funny.

"We had to know you were okay."

Was I? I wondered. I could think and I could move. Right? I twitched both my feet, just to be sure. There was a bandage on the side of my neck and on my chest, but I wasn't hooked to as many machines now as earlier.

She brushed back my hair. "You'll be fine," she said. "I told you that you didn't die."

"Nobody died."

"I'm so glad."

"What about Smoke?"

She smiled and nodded. "We got her back."

I was so glad and relieved. I was also so stupid with fatigue, I could barely stay awake. "Too bad I can't be there," I murmured.

"It's safer here," she replied. Then the reality of what had happened hit and we both grimaced. She leaned close and kissed me. Pulling back, she said, "I can't believe what you did," she said quietly.

I knew what she meant. I was proud of what I'd done and I hoped she was proud of me.

"We were watching. We all just looked at each other and then back at the screen. Cutter! Oh, my God, Matt. I can't believe you asked for Cutter.

"He doesn't seem like the world's worst guy."

"That took us all by surprise."

"I think he really liked Smoke."

She nodded. "She knew he was setting her free when he came into the room and released her hands."

When he nuzzled her ear.

"He told her you had the poison," she said

"I wonder what happened after she vanished," I said.

"I don't know. All I know is that The Foundation will never give up looking for Smoke. She made fools of them twice."

"What about Teddy?"

"He's still recovering, but he'll be fine."

"And Gabe?"

She hesitated. "Nothing more has been said about Cres Singledon but I *know* that Daniel is not the bad guy. He couldn't be any more than I could or you could. Or Smoke or Gabe or Dairy or Aiden. It's not possible. I know his heart."

"Sirena, those people … being tortured—"

She burst into a glorious smile. "We got them!"

My heart did a wild loop-de-loop in my chest. "For real?"

She nodded emphatically. "We were watching and Ji was going crazy. So was Aiden. They knew some of those people. So, Ji had this idea and he and Dom started working on it. The rest of us were glued to what you were doing and saying, but they went after everyone with training. We'd already locked in the coordinates of the room, thanks to you, so the second we got Smoke back, we directed enough energy to it to overload their circuits and then we transferred a team in."

I could picture it. It would have been thrilling and crazy dangerous. Then my blood ran a little cold. "You went, didn't you?" I asked, suddenly sure that she had.

"Oh, you are not going to get self-righteous on me. After what you put me through? Besides, it went perfectly."

But what if it hadn't? What if she'd been caught? But before I could say anything else, I felt a warning tingle and Sirena faded right before my eyes. It was just for a moment, and then she was back. But we were out of time.

She leaned forward and pressed another kiss to my lips. "I can't wait until you're back."

"Me, too." There was a knock at the door, I glanced over and, in that split second, Sirena was gone.

"How we doing?" a nurse asked as she came in.

Damn her. I knew she was just doing her job but damn her for costing even one split second of being with Sirena.

She checked my temperature, blood pressure and respiration. "Do you need anything?"

Sirena, I thought. "Can I get a soda?"

"Of course."

It's too bad I was asleep again before she came back with it.

21

Cres

It took more than a week before I began to feel like myself again. No visitors had been allowed except for Mom, but flowers and notes kept arriving. Ty snuck in once, but they caught him before he even made it halfway across the room. Still, it brightened my day, especially when he smuggled in a gift from 'the gang', a new Ipod. They created a playlist of music featuring a hero theme, songs like Lookin' for a Hero by Bonnie Tyler and Go The Distance by Michael Bolton and Heart of Hero by Luther Vandross. Way corny stuff. That isn't to say I haven't listened to every bit of it with a goofy smile on my face.

My cell phone was confiscated until I'm stronger. I asked how strong you have to be to text but didn't get an answer. I grumbled about Big Brother, but no one cared.

I wasn't complaining about anything because I now had an understanding of how lucky I was. I was shot in the chest, near my right shoulder, and the side of my head and neck was 'grazed,' but if two of the three bullets had hit a fraction of an inch over, I wouldn't have made it. The chest wound was the most serious injury, but it during the vascular repair of the neck wound, or more accurately stated, 'the zone two injury of the neck, second degree GSW,' which stands for gunshot wound, that my pulse dropped so low, they thought they'd lost me. I wonder if that's when I passed out leaving the maze.

One positive development is that moving to Charlotte is off the table. Now the plan is for us to stay in town and move in with Dave. Moving to Charlotte is a good long term move for his career, but he says it can be put off for another year so I can finish school here. He's a good guy.

"Gee whiz, look at the flowers."

I grinned with delight to see Graylin in the doorway. "I know. Right?" I fumbled with the TV remote to get it off. Let us just say, my coordination is not what it was. "There were even more. From total strangers. The nurses distributed them around to patients who didn't have any."

She stuck her backpack against the far wall and came and sat in the chair beside my bed. "So, how are you feeling today?" she asked with mock solicitousness.

"Better every day, thank you," I answered in the same overly proper, just shy of smart-ass manner.

"Do you know they wouldn't let me in to see you? Me! Badge and all."

"No respect for the law anymore," I sympathized. "It's just sad."

She smirked. "How's physical therapy going?"

"I've got movement issues with my right arm. Severely limited strength and a serious lack of coordination. But my physical therapist tells me that I'm, and I quote, getting there."

"Good," she replied enthusiastically. "You know, your mom is having a field day with interviews."

I shook my head. "Far as I'm concerned, she can have her fifteen minutes of fame and mine, too."

Graylin made a face. "I'm not sure it will be that easy. There's been a lot of speculation about you."

I moaned. "Not the speculation thing again."

She shrugged. "It seems your lot in life. Although now it's, 'who is this Mighty Matt Matthews,'" she said in an affected voice.

I blinked. "Mighty Matt Matthews?" I repeated.

She nodded and looked pained. "Courtesy of Ty. He claims it's your nickname. Triple M, short for—"

"Mighty Matt Matthews," we finished together.

She chuckled. "I have to admit, it was news to me."

I smiled, both entertained and relieved. "Me, too."

There was a knock on the door and we looked over to see a nurse standing there. "Ten minutes," she said to Graylin.

"But I just got here," Graylin complained. "And I'm the law."

The nurse rolled her eyes and walked off.

Graylin gave me a pouty look.

"I know," I said. "Big Brother. Somebody ought to report this place."

"You just can't beat the man. Can I smuggle you in some contraband next time I come?"

"But that's illegal and you don't do illegal."

"I meant like a Snickers bar or a hamburger and onion rings kind of thing."

"All of it sounds pretty good."

"Done. Of course, if I fall into a life of crime now, we'll both know who's to blame."

"Speaking of crime, what's going on with the case?"

"Well, they're not breaking the brat squad up yet." She made a goofy face and clapped factiously. "Yay! I get to go on being in high school. Forever. Or until we catch this freak. Whichever comes first."

"Dora wasn't caught?"

"No, she was. I meant the main bad guy. Eudora Blake is in custody and I'm pretty sure she'll be tried as an adult and end up an el-wop."

"A what?"

"Life without chance of parole. The abbreviation is L-WOP."

I felt a myriad of mixed emotions. There may have even been some pity there. "The day of the shooting—"

"Yeah?"

"I thought I heard gunfire from somewhere else in the school."

She cringed. "*That* was near catastrophe. See, when you texted, I called a full-scale alert. Cops came running not to mention the fire department, ambulances, the DEA. Well, there happened to be this cruiser close by with a rookie cop in it and they arrived first. They came in a back door with weapons drawn. This is just as some band kids were rushing back to their classes because of the announcement. This one kid had a clarinet in hand and, I don't know, the way he was holding it."

"Oh, no."

She nodded. "The rookie thought it was a weapon and took aim. Luckily, his partner saw what was happening and barreled into him."

"Oh, geez."

"The gun discharged, but no one was hurt."

It was crazy how shaken I was by the description. It put me back there, and back there was a stressful place to be.

She stood. "So, before Nurse Killjoy comes back and hauls me out of here, I have something for you."

"Oh, yeah?"

"Yeah." nShe went and got the backpack, opened it and pulled out a good-sized wrapped box. "A present."

"What's this for?" I asked as she came toward me. She handed it over and it had some weight to it.

"Cause," she replied.

"Cause?"

"Cause you are a really great guy, and 'cause you were instrumental to the investigation. And 'cause the bureau paid for it. It's from all us brats with great admiration and affection."

Grinning ear to ear, I tore into the bright blue and green striped wrapping paper, but stopped when I recognized what it was. "A laptop?"

She beamed that famous smile of hers. "A good one. You'll need one for school, anyway, so—"

"You guys got me a laptop?"

"Yeah, a good one. You'll need one for school anyway. Hey, didn't we just have this conversation?"

I was totally blown away. "I don't know what to say."

"You don't have to say anything. It's a thank you for all you did. And I know, you don't think you did all that much. Except you did."

"Oh, man," I said, completely overwhelmed.

Graylin kept beaming. Not even Nurse Killjoy clearing her throat at the door wiped the smile off her face. I still couldn't believe I was holding a brand new, state of the art laptop. "Thank you! I mean, really. Thank you. Will you tell everyone I said thank you?"

"I will. And I'll call you tomorrow." She leaned over and kissed my cheek. "I'm so glad you're better."

"Thanks."

She left, only pausing to grab her book bag and give Nurse Killjoy a sweet smile. "Bye, Sherlock," she called to me.

"See ya, Watson."

After she left, I pulled out the light-weight computer, knowing I'd never owned anything as nice. I tried connecting to the internet and it connected. I'd never been wireless before. Nor had my email ever held as much. I had two hundred and fourteen messages in my inbox and even more than that in my junk mail. My eyes just about bulged out of my head. One by one, I started through them. There were emails from every person I knew, plus a lot I didn't know. They were wishing me well, thanking me, and calling me a hero. How had they gotten my email address?

As soon as my eyes lit on one from JaniceC@MarshSingledon.com, I opened it.

Dear Matt,
I'm the head of marketing at Marsh-Singledon and will be happy to provide information for your senior project. Please forward your questions. We appreciate you being a fan of Ruaun3.

I thought about it and then wrote back.

Dear Ms. C,
Thank you for your response. I was hoping to get in touch with Cres Singledon. I believe I know his twin brothers. If you could pass that on to him, I would really appreciate it.
Thanks again,
Matt Matthews

First thing, the following morning, I got on my laptop and discovered several new emails, including one from Janice C. In it, she suggested I must be mistaken about Singledon, because he had no family to speak of. She then repeated her offer to help with my project and wished me a good day.

I wrote her back stating that I was certain of my information and repeating my desire to have the message passed on. If she didn't mind, I said. It was really important, I said. And, by the way, I hoped she had a good day, too.

She wrote right back; we're practically talking instant messaging here, asking if I was the same guy that had been involved in the school shooting in North Carolina. I replied that I was, and then I waited, staring expectantly at the screen, but she didn't write back.

I spent the next few hours in physical therapy and, afterwards I took a walk through just about every hospital corridor. Sweating, grunting, occasionally fighting bouts of dizziness, pushing. I was being released in a few days, so I needed to get all I could out of PT while I had it.

I was worn out and mindlessly surfing TV channels that evening when the sound of a man clearing his throat made me look over at the door. *Whoa.* Cres Singledon was standing there.

"Matt?"

"Yes! Come in." I turned off the TV as fast as my fumbling hands would allow.

He walked closer and offered his hand. "Cres Singledon."

It took effort to shake it. My right arm isn't performing like it did before. "I know," I said. "I recognize you."

"You recognize me?"

"I saw a picture on the internet."

"Oh." He gestured to a chair. "May I?"

"Please." He sat and I brought the head of my bed up higher. "I guess you got the message I sent."

"I did, yes. It confused me a bit. A mention of …
brothers?"

He said it like it was a quasi-preposterous notion. So that's the way we were going to play it. I nodded. "There's a strong resemblance. Actually, the picture on the internet wasn't very clear. It's really through your brothers that I recognize you."

"Who, exactly, are you talking about?"

"Gabe and Westin. I've met them. I've been there."

"Been where?"

"I think you know where."

He didn't speak for a moment. "I don't," he finally said with a shrug.

"Ruaun3."

Cres smiled as if I was being amusing, but it wasn't convincing. "Okay," he said, as if I was a whack job. "Was this after you were shot?"

"Before and after. I'll happily tell you how it all happened on my end, but I can't tell you why it happened. I was hoping you could tell me that."

He still had this half smile on his face that suggested I was off my rocker. He opened his arms. "Go ahead."

I took a breath and exhaled. "I've played the game for years and loved it. It's been my escape."

"That's good to hear. According to the articles I read, you're a straight A student."

"Yes, but school's always come easy. Anyway, I always had a thing for Sirena. A crush, you could say."

He nodded. "I get it. She's a desirable character. The designers have done an awesome job creating her."

"I agree. And that's all I thought it was. Sometimes I dreamt of her, but not like the dream I had a few months ago. It was a weird warning dream. Then, right after that, I saw her at school. She was sitting right next to me in honors History during a supremely boring educational film on the fall of the Roman empire. She was just there a second and then she was gone."

"Uh-huh."

"I know," I said, fully getting his skepticism. "I thought I was losing it at the time. I went home and looked up mental illness on the internet."

Cres grinned and seemed to relax a little.

"That's how I stumbled across hypnosis, self-hypnosis, which I tried. And it worked. I worked myself into a trance where I saw her ... and some other stuff."

"Uh-huh," he said again.

"I know how it sounds, but I *have* been there. The first time, it happened through that self-hypnosis session, but the next times were different. Once Sirena showed up in my room and brought me back. This last go-round, I found myself with Sirena and Gabe, and we were watching some kind of raid going on. There were these bizarre red lines of light."

There was suddenly concern in his face, and we're not just talking a flicker.

"It was a detection and containment field. See? I'm not lying. I met people there who aren't part of the game. Like Dom and Glass."

Cres's respiration increased.

"I've been in Sirena's lodge. I can describe it to you in detail. I've been in RU2. I know about the sensors imbedded in their palms to open doors. Gabe joked they had all sorts of hidden compartments. I know about the poison, naira. I know about the tiers. I even know some things that you don't know, like that Teddy got picked up in a raid and Smoke went into the maze after him. I've been there, too."

He'd paled. "It's not possible," he stammered.

"Sirena told me she used to be in a tier, but there was an explosion and three of them were killed."

He shook his head. "I don't believe this."

"I think you do," I said carefully. "If you don't, I'll keep going."

He rose and paced around before stopping in back of the chair which he gripped hard. "I must have blazed a traceable path. What else could it be? It has to be that." He walked to the door and then turned back to me. "Do you mind if I shut this?"

"No."

He closed the door and walked back to the chair, choosing to stand behind it again. "Sirena was your first contact?"

I was glad the pretense was over. "Yes."

"So, when you saw her, what did you say? What did she say?"

"It's like we already knew one another. Later she told me our energy has connected for years, but she was surprised that I was … you know, actually there. To be honest, that first time she was pissed about it. She said it was too dangerous for me, especially when she hadn't bridged me over."

Cres wasn't looking so good.

"The time she came for me was to talk about the game."

Cres exhaled in a rush. "They know about the game?"

"Yeah. I told them."

He looked off, adjusting to this info. "Shit."

"Sirena believes we're psylinks."

"Well, that's impossible, Matt," he said tiredly. He came around and sat back down again, leaning forward, elbows to knees. "However difficult life may be here and now, it's nothing compared to what happens in the future. I realize I'm saying that knowing what you—" He gestured to the equipment around me. "—just experienced. I'm sorry it happened. From what I read, it could have been a lot worse except for you. But my point is that as things get really bad here, humans change. In the centuries still to come, some of the population will develop pronounced psychic and kinetic abilities as a matter of survival."

I nodded. "Like Smoke is DEC."

Cres blanched. "Jesus Christ, Matt. How many times have you been there?"

"Three. But the first time, I didn't know what was going on or even if it was real. The second time, I saw more; I knew it was real, but I couldn't stay long. This last time … I stayed longer. That's when I was—"

"Shot," he supplied under his breath. "Unconscious."

"Yes. But right before I was out, I thought of her and we think she thought of me that exact same instant. Our energy must have done the … thing. The bridging."

He stared, trying to come to terms with what I'd told him. "I can't understand going back and forth so freely. It shouldn't be possible."

"Don't you do it?"

His eyes flashed. "I spent more than a decade making it happen," he snapped. "And I have the technology. Technology that I created."

"No. You're right. I'm sorry. That sounded flippant. I didn't mean it that way, I swear."

"No, I'm sorry," he relented. "This has just—" he broke off, struggling for the right words.

"Blown your mind?"

"Yes. It changes everything."

"How?"

"I … don't know yet."

A moment of uncomfortable silence fell between us.

He shook his head slowly. "I didn't think it was possible."

"You don't know how grateful I am that it is. I kind of feel like I belong there more than here."

"Oh, Matt," he said with a shake of his head. "No."

I'd spoken the truth but I didn't have the energy to convince him. Nor did I feel the need. "Well, whatever the answers are, I have it on good authority that you're the man. Sirena said you created a lot of the technology that they depend on. That you're brilliant. That is, I heard *Daniel* was brilliant."

"Sirena," he said with a wistful smile. "She was a prodigy."

I grinned. "Yeah?"

"Yeah."

There was a rap at the door. The nurse had opened it without me noticing. "Wrap it up, gentlemen," she said before walking on.

Crap. I had a million questions for him. "Can I ask, how did you find this time and place? Or did you find it on purpose."

"Not exactly. No." He leaned back. "I've always been obsessed with wormholes. Are you into physics?"

"I'm interested in it. But I thought wormholes were a thing of fiction. That's the current thinking. That they're hypothetical."

"I know. And they're rare. We've developed instrumentation that makes identification of them possible, but it's still a tedious endeavor. If you are fortunate enough to come across one, you have to lock onto the coordinates immediately or you might never find it again. I found *this* one when I was nineteen. In fact, I found it so easily; I didn't fully realize the miracle of it. I would learn, of course. I'd learn a great many things." He turned his head slightly and pointed to a crescent shaped scar on the side of his face. "That was a lesson from the first time I ricocheted."

That's where the Cres had come from. No wonder Westin had realized who it was. It was probably a nickname they had come up with. "Ricocheted?"

"To go back and forth. It's a long explanation but first I built a vessel to traverse the wormhole. At least that was the idea. That took four plus years. When I thought we were ready for trial runs, I programmed the T-Cor, that's what I called it, to send and return a subject. Let's just say the subsequent experiments did not go well, so we reworked calculations again and again."

"We," I said.

"I had a staff. Have a staff, I suppose. There is a small planet designated for research and academic pursuit."

"Rowan-Backna?" I recalled.

He blinked. "Bachna," he corrected.

I seemed to have thrown him. "Reworked calculations," I coaxed.

"Once I thought we finally had it right," he began again, "—some two and half years later, I decided to try it myself. By that point, it was an obsession. At first, I just ricocheted. It would take years and a few failed experiments before I had the courage for a one-way trip."

206

"One-way," I repeated.

"Yes. When you make a leap like that, you cannot possibly know you'll get back. After all this time, I still can't know for sure. So I planned for a one-way trip, but I made it back again. So it ended up being round trip. I never even donned a stitch of clothes."

"I want to hear every single thing about it," I said.

He nodded. "When we have the time and privacy, I'm amenable. But we're almost out of both so I need to ask you something."

"Sure Anything."

"Is there something you want from me?"

Did he think I wanted to blackmail him or something? "Just to understand it as best as I can."

He studied me for a couple of seconds and then nodded. "Okay."

"How long has it been since you've gone back?"

"More than a year."

"Things are not good. The raids—"

"Are nothing new," he interrupted. "If The Foundation wasn't so greedy with their tendrils spread out to scores of different planets, they would have already claimed total possession of Ruaun3. They have the capability to do it. Think back on the Nazis at the height of their power and then give them atomic weaponry, E-bombs, autonomous weapons, masers. The Foundation is that ruthless and powerful. They've underestimated our will and fortitude, but they won't forever.

"You make it sound hopeless."

He shrugged and shook his head. "I wish I didn't believe it was. But I've seen what they do. I'm not my brothers or Smoke or Aiden or any of the others. I would choose for them to go elsewhere. Or to come here. Leave Ruaun3 to the damned Foundation. It's not worth the cost."

It was such a grim view, it depressed me. "Sirena said you'd helped."

"Well, of course, I helped. I'll always help as much as I can. But I won't give it my life. And if I could talk my brothers or Sirena or any of them out of that life, I would."

"Can you … go anytime?" I asked, stammering a little, because this question was so important to me.

He hesitated a moment. "Yes."

"And when you're there, you can stay as long as you want?" I said, nodding with hopefulness. "Not that I'm asking to go, but … you do have the ability to transport somebody else, right?"

"Do I have the ability? Yes. Would I assume that responsibility?" He paused and then shook his head. "No. The risks are too high. Simply because I've managed to go back and forth several times, doesn't mean that the next time won't be the last. Things go wrong. In fact, it's always more likely that something will go wrong than that everything will go right. And no one would ever know what became of me. Think about that for a moment. I face that fear and accept the risk every time I go. Every time I go there and every time I return here."

And then Nurse Killjoy appeared with her customary frown. "Visiting hours are over," she stated.

"Just a little while more," I begged. "Please?"

"It's okay, Matt," Cres said as he stood. He reached into his pocket for a business card and handed it to me. "My number and email are written on back. We'll talk more soon."

I felt like whining like a three-year old because I had so many more questions and I needed him to understand how deeply I felt about everything and everyone on Ruaun3. It wasn't *just* that I loved a girl there. Although, there was that.

"I know," he said. "We didn't even scratch the surface yet. Would you be interested in visiting me when you're discharged?"

"Yes!"

"Good. I'll arrange it when you're ready. For now, take care. Get well." He held out his hand.

I shook it. "Thank you for coming."

He nodded and left. For I don't how long, I sat there going over and over everything he'd said. Excitement kept surging up and catching in my chest because no matter what he'd said about assuming responsibility for my safety, there was now a way of going and staying in Ruaun3 for a substantial period of time. Maybe even forever.

I got out of bed and made my way to the window. I looked past my reflected image to the colorful headlights and taillights of traffic below. It's easy to have a grand perspective from that kind of vantage point. It's tougher when you're sitting in class, bored out of your mind. Or sitting in the car in stop and go traffic just trying to get home after a long day, especially knowing that tomorrow is another one you'll have to get through. I guess it's all about perspective.

I looked up at the faint stars and felt a surge of exhilaration again because I'm going back. Somehow, some way, I'm going back.

It's been an interesting few months, and what I've learned is this. Everything comes down to the choices you make. I'm excited about the choices ahead, even the tough ones. Especially the tough ones. Oh, and there's one more truth I've accepted. I am *not* invisible.

About the Author

Jane Shoup (Super) is an award-winning author of more than twenty books in several different genres. (The product of a big imagination and a short attention span.) She lives in Greensboro, North Carolina (not far from Matt) with her husband, Scott, their rescue, Gabby, and near her adult daughters and their families, including a half dozen grands ranging in age from one to ten-going-on-fifteen. Get togethers are frequent, noisy, and chaotic.

Visit her website at www.janeshoup.com